Behold the continuing mar

Tales of New A

Volume 2

A deconstructed Steampunk novella in seven short stories,
two memoir extracts and a play.

Conceived and written by Daren Callow.

Illuminated and graphitized by Frog Morris (again).

1st Edition – November 2019

Dedicated to Alfie Phoenix, who came into this world a whole lot quicker than this second volume.

A Monkey Teaspoon Publication.

For sure this time.

Or is it?

Yes, it definitely is.

Probably.

ISBN 9781707634255

To comprehend further the lunacy herewithin, please attend:

www.talesofnewalbion.com

Without These Fine Folk
All This Would Not Be Half As Good

To all the wonderful folk who attended readings, commented, read, listened and allowed me to write in their establishments. Most especially to Surrey Steampunk Convivial, Surrey; Coffee Station, Hove; The Garden Bar, Hove and the Yellow Book, Brighton. To Nils "Smugglers, what smugglers? Tis all free traders here" Visser, Ben "Cubinoid" Henderson, Darren Gooding, Lynda Savigar, Tudor Davies, Mary Savigar, Anniken Haga, Chris Plummer, James Percy, Jessica Szturmann and Frog & Vikki Morris for encouragement, friendship and (where applicable) on-going creative collaboration. To Steve Jones, the Steampunk DJ, for lobbing the Hamster & Gecko grenade at me (not literally).

I am much obliged to Emma King, Catherine Paver, Frog Morris, Professor Elemental, Mikey Georgeson, Peter Gardiner and Ben and Tixia Henderson for their contributions to the ARC Light Programme.

Last, but almost certainly not least, so much love and thanks to my charming, beautiful wife and muse – Charlie Savigar.

More Before Words

Mister Daren Callow is a writer I hold in great esteem; which is no mean trick I can assure you, for I am slave to that infuriating tendency, common in most playwrights and poets, to pick politely, but obsessively away at others' work, (although perhaps with not quite the same masochistic glee as one does at one's own) and not desist from detailed analysis until one has comprehensively sucked every mote of joy and laughter from each narrative nook and comedic cranny. However, Mister Callow achieves that rare thing to which all comedy must aspire; he makes it appear effortless.

As has been bitterly pointed out by many an undervalued Stand Up; 'Comedy isn't bleeding easy you know!' Though I will not go as far as to say it is 'the hardest job in the world', for I do not wish my esteemed literary friend to be immediately inundated with letters of complaint from respectable quantum physicists, complaining that coming up with a functional rule of three gag is a piece of cake besides Robertson–Schrödinger uncertainty relations, (whilst of course simultaneously NOT being a piece of cake besides Robertson–Schrödinger uncertainty relations). That notwithstanding, an adventure comedy is more difficult than it appears, because not only does it have to deal with all the exposition, inciting incidents, complications, reveals, reversals, climaxes and resolutions, which such plots require to function satisfactorily, it also has to make you laugh. This is not unlike asking a builder to construct a perfectly functional kitchen extension, which meets all the building regulations, but to also insist he constructs it in a witty and amusing fashion, with at least three jokes per joist.

I first encountered Daren Callow in 2015 at the Surrey Steampunk Convivial; reading the very first story in what was to become 'Tales of New Albion: Volume One'. I beheld a slim, tallish man with a close-clipped beard, sporting suit trousers and waistcoat, with a silver tie, (the man that is, not the beard). He was sitting before a microphone, reading animatedly from a sheaf of typed A4 to an audience of splendidly attired individuals, within the upstairs function room of the Royal Oak Pub in New Maldon. I sat down to hear the story he was relating and almost five years, and twenty stories later I remain eager to devour every new instalment of Daren Callow's work.

Like his portfolio, Mister Callow's following is ever growing through numerous live readings, podcasts and the publication of Volume One of his tales. So, what has changed? Well, his suit is now adorned with a smidgeon more additional Steampunk badges, cogs and wondrous fripperies and there is perhaps a touch more grey in his beard, but the rattling adventures continue unabated.

As a book, these stories read incredibly well, which is largely I suspect because they have been read incredibly well, (aloud, by the author, at this procession of different Surrey Convivials). Let it also be noted that Daren is a fine performer in his own right and an accomplished voice artist. I have witnessed his captivated audience; listening in delight and rocking with laughter at his turns of phrase and narrative. He does not tend to go "script free", or fully physically inhabit his characters in the manner of an actor performing a one man show, but his readings are dynamic and animated; often replete with frantic arm waving; particularly when reporting the speech of perpetually flustered inventor Sir Grenville Lushthorpe.

I am aware some listeners of audio books and podcasts prefer their narrators to not attempt 'voices', as they can disparagingly put it. Some prefer all characters read uniformly with the narrator's natural voice, but as someone from a theatre background I take an unashamed delight in an author who can turn on a dime between different characters and be in the space of as many lines; a gravel voiced cockney mercenary, a roaring upper-class buffoon and an earnest young lady. All these personas Daren Callow manages with aplomb.

Daren's stories are an inviting bag of individually wrapped, easily digestible delights which also link together into a grander, more ambitious narrative, that like it's component parts possesses a Beginning, a Middle and an End, (which arrive beguilingly, like Morecambe's Grieg, not necessarily in the right order). They are best read as individual shorts; I recommend you don't gorge on this book cover to cover, though you may be tempted as they are terribly moreish, but enjoy them for the intricate little treats that they are.

These stories sit within a universe which one could generally described as 'Steampunk', but let's not get into what exactly is 'Steampunk'; for as has been noted by observers wiser than I, if one asks 10 different Steampunks to describe 'what is Steampunk' one shall be rewarded with 11 different conflicting definitions. Sufficed to say, this is a Victorian world of airships, aquatic rockets and all manner of steam-powered contraptions and automata.

Comparisons could be made to Douglas Adams or Terry Pratchett, in terms of Callow's overall comedic world building, (or should that be 'universe' building; there is a Martian war on after all), but there is also a touch of Milligan's inspired 'Goon Show' lunacy and Croft and Perry's 'Dad's Army' wistful sitcom comedy about the eccentric inadequacies of his characters. There is a delightful, self-depreciating Britishness about this rogues gallery; New Albion is an agreeably recognisable world, full of ageing military idiots, gung-ho public school politicians, well meaning, but self-important scientists and terribly nice, but often highly inexperienced, young things trying jolly hard to do their best (despite being hideously out of their depth in an adventure which continues to spiral wildly out of control). Few are wholly reputable, but less still are truly unpleasant, save perhaps for the odious Mister Snook...

I have not enquired how Callow writes, whether his descriptive bon mots drop from a nib as effortlessly as notes dashed off by

Schaffer's Mozart, or whether each silly name is agonized over like Michelangelo slaving beneath the ceiling of the Sistine Chapel, but however Daren creates, the results feel blithe and delightful. It is a pleasure to encounter these stories on the page and whether dear potential reader you arc flipping through this foreword in some delightful little independent bookshop, or perusing a free sample on your portable, personal telephonic device, courtesy of Mister A. Mazon esquire, I heartily recommend you vacillate no longer and purchase this fine volume.

Despite being cruelly brought forth into this world with only one functional 'R' to his name, Daren has battled on triumphantly; overcoming his alphabetic handicap to become an author of note. In Volume Two of this fine series you shall encounter the endearingly discombobulated Rusty Inglemop, as she battles the Heath Robinson like 'Hot Desking' of the Monkey Teaspoon Design Agency, and the self-aggrandising autobiographical ramblings of Theodore Pilkington-Rhubarb; Continuity Announcer for the Albion Radiophonic Corporation. We also have the return of beloved characters in the form of, amongst others, Sir Grenville Lushthorpe, alongside cynical disgruntled mercenary Tobias Fitch, the ever-resourceful Ellen Hall and, of course space cat Mrs. Tickle III. (Did I mention I adore silly names?)

Now, read on...

Darren Gooding, *Darkest Essex, November 2019*

What Lies Onwards

XI

Monkey Teaspoon Design Agency

Rusty Inglemop was late for work and it was making her a bit anxious. It was bad enough that the first Lanchester Central omnitram had been crammed to the seams, but the second to arrive only had standing room on the third floor. Rusty had hoped to arrive at work ready for anything, but in her least shoddy slacks and over-polished work shoes, she now felt only hot and flustered. Not the perfect way to kick off her first day at the best design agency in town, nay the whole country, although no one in the metropolis would ever concede this point. This was just one of the reasons why she was so keen to get a position here, but also why she was so desperate to make a good impression on her first day. Rounding the corner to Cecil Street, dodging nimbly to miss the commuters hurrying this way and that she got her first glimpse of the magnificently modern two-storey building that in gleaming two-foot-high brass letters with incandescent lightbulbs boldly declared itself to be the "Monkey Teaspoon Design Agency".

The Agency was indeed renown across the whole of the land but since it was located in New Albion's second city, it was afflicted with a certain inferiority complex that led it to grab any chance to show off. One of these opportunities for bragging rights was through it's incredible state-of-the-art travelling hot desk system, which ran over two floors and was the envy of every civilized bit of the globe. She had been warned in no uncertain terms that it was imperative to arrive between 8:47 and 9:08 to make her desk allocation, the consequences of missing this foreboding departure time made her shiver inside as finally she made it to the agency gates and looked around desperately for her rendezvous. She had been told to report to the clocking-in machine where one of the under-designers in her team would be there to show her the ropes. Glancing this way and that as she skipped up the marble staircase to the gleaming lobby, she plumped for the complicated looking machine with three clock faces (alarmingly reading six minutes past nine in glorious triplicate!) and racks of paper cards either side indicating all those in the two hundred strong workforce who were in, or indeed yet to arrive. Waiting patiently for her under the eccentric contraption was a young lady with slightly dishevelled red hair and old-fashioned spectacles, holding a card and glancing with seemingly equal nervousness in all directions. As Rusty approached the lady's face lit up with hope, if not actual delight, and she proffered a clammy hand.

'You must be Inglemop, I'm Arkwright, you can call me Nancy though.' She almost found a smile as they shook hands somewhat perfunctory.

'Inglemop, yes... er Rusty really, y'know, good to...erm you know, likewise,' garbled Rusty taking the piece of card that Nancy had in her other hand, which was neatly embossed with the words "R. Tingledrop".

'You cut it a bit fine Rusty, insert here,' Nancy pointed to a slot in the oak and brass contraption and before Rusty could utter one syllable of complaint about the misspelling of her name the machine sucked the card out of her hand and started clattering and chuntering vigorously. Then, after various clockwork mechanisms had finished their work, with the ding of a tiny bell, and a two-tone whistle, the card was expelled back into Rusty's sweaty paw. She glanced down to see that it was neatly stamped "09:07:58".

'Oh gosh that's all jolly precise, erm time, you know,' blurted Rusty as Nancy guided her to pop the card into a vacant slot in the right-hand rack.

'You just made it! Better crack on though as we need to get a desk with our team or there will be no end of troubles.' And so, with still not a window of opportunity to mention the name issues, they were on their way from clocking-in to filing with barely a breath in between.

It was only a short hop, skip and jump to filing, but in that brief time Nancy filled her in a little on her new team.

'I'm deputy vice leader of Underlining Team B,' she began as she strode purposefully ahead. 'You'll probably be on something simple today, like dotting Is, but it will all be in your notes.' As she followed behind Rusty could not help but admire Nancy's natty utility belt with setsquares, rulers and various fountain pens arranged by size. It did rather make her battered wooden pencil case look a bit middle school, and she made a mental note to upgrade herself at the first pay cheque. This was assuming they decided to keep her at all, her first day was not going quite as she'd visualised it whilst failing to fall asleep last night. There was not time for further reflection however, as they arrived in "Filing" and Rusty was mildly surprised to find that the counter was attended by a bookish looking older gentleman with apron and steel eyepieces and a medium-sized primate with similar apron (albeit smaller) and a flat cap, sucking laconically on a brass spoon attached to a chain around its neck. Before she could say anything other than a small gurgle, the primate had ducked under the counter to retrieve Nancy's wheeled filing drawers and push them out to her. The man, clearly identifying Rusty as so-new-it-hurt, reached for a clipboard.

'Name?' he enquired without looking up.

'Inglemop,' ventured Rusty optimistically and then felt her face redden as the clerk flicked back and forth amongst his typed sheets of foolscap with no success.

'Erm, I might be under Tingledrop, but that's not really...' the man cut her short with a raised hand and continued to flick his papers. The tension was palpable and glancing at the nonplussed primate who was sucking on his spoon again whilst waiting for his next assignment, she decided to try and crack the ice.

'Ah,' she gurgled and pointed, without really thinking, 'Monkey. Teaspoon. Eh?' With this, the animal gave her the dirtiest stare she had ever received in all her days, the spoon dropping from his mouth in sheer disgust at the statement, and then it turned and walked out of the booth. Even the clerk and Arkwright looked at her slack jawed. 'Oh flipperations, what have I er, oh gosh,' garbled Rusty incoherently.

'He's not too happy with you,' muttered the clerk sternly, 'anyone with eyes can see he's an ape, not a monkey.'

'Oh gosh to goodness, I am so...' but she was cut off again as the man finally found her name on his sheet.

'Tingledrop – 231!' called out the clerk loudly so the departed chimp could hear in the filing room. 'The tail is the giveaway,' he added.

'What tail?' burbled Rusty, feeling that she was glowing red so much it was probably illuminating the whole room.

'Precisely!' added the clerk as a set of filing drawers was shoved roughly out of the back room and Rusty realised that she had better grab them and get a move on.

'Oh, I really am so, so sorry,' pleaded Rusty bending down to call under the counter towards the sulking ape. 'I'm not a speciesist or anything, honestly, I'm...'

'We need to go!' snapped Nancy from the doorway her front already turned and her back retreating down the corridor.

'Right, oh, gosh, so sorry again,' muttered Rusty grabbing the drawers and wheeling them out after her. The clerk shook his head sternly as they departed.

'In any case that was obviously a dessert spoon,' he chuntered to himself, but the ladies were already out of earshot.

Kicking herself mentally in the rear for her primate related faux pas, Rusty suddenly had to swerve hard to avoid a collision. An oriental looking lady in a smart silk waistcoat accompanied by two burly men in long trench coats and hats pulled low over their eyes had stormed around the corner without looking. They were clearly heading for the filing room and they didn't care who they had to trample on to get there.

'Mind out the way!' snarled one of the men and Rusty could do little other than mumble a pathetic,

'Sorry' before they were gone. Gosh, she thought to herself sarcastically, could they be any more suspicious?

But she could not dwell on the rude strangers further as she began to hear the rumblings of the famous hot desk transit system, used exclusively by Monkey Teaspoon to the covetousness of many a bigger design agency in the metropolis. The complicated system worked by employing a series of conveyor belts carrying one-person personal desk platforms on rails around the building and as she rounded the final corner to the departure platform Rusty could see this amazing contraption in action for the first time. Each personal unit was equipped with a drafting desk, an adjustable chair (heated), angle-poise lamp and complicated telephonic system with wires and dials going down to the conveying mountings on the floor. Finally, each little unit had an area to clamp one's filing cabinet and, for this purpose, the mechanism caused the contraptions to lift off the belts and pause briefly at a ramp configuration so that each employee in turn could push their cabinet into position and jump aboard. With consummate ease of one seasoned in such things Nancy locked her drawers into place and jumped aboard as the desk that was clearly intended for Rusty chuntered and clicked into the raised loading position.

'Oh crikey!' jabbered Rusty in mild panic as the little train confronted her and she shoved her drawers with all her might up onto the little platform and then clung on for grim death as the little carriage unlocked from the ramp, dropped onto the rails and began to move off on the conveyor belt into the building.

'Good work,' praised Nancy from the desk ahead, 'you'll soon get used to it all.' After this she proceeded to show her how a pair of pedals under the desk could be used to close up on the desk ahead or drop back to the one following. This way desks could be bunched up for meetings or to enable two colleagues to confer. For everything else there was a little rolodex and the telephone system to call other people in the building. Nancy showed her how to plug in her personal number using the matrix and copper routing cables provided.

'You're all set I think,' suggested Nancy, 'take a look in your top drawer and you should have today's assignment, probably something very simple to get you started.'

Doing as she was bid and taking care to keep her balance as the desk continued to trundle its way along the slightly uneven rails, Rusty opened the drawer and then immediately slammed it tightly shut. Instead of the expected paperwork and instructions, the top drawer instead contained a single foolscap folder labelled, in no uncertain terms (and block capitals) HOMELAND SECURITY – TOPMOST SECRET PLANS – HIGHEST CLEARANCE ONLY – OR ELSE!! Rusty gulped hard and gingerly pulled open the drawer slightly to make sure there was no mistake, but there really wasn't. There had obviously been some terrible error, and it didn't take long for her to work out what it was. The number on her drawer's little brass plaque, which she only became aware of now, read 232 and not 231. The filing chimp, in his fit of pique or just because he hated her guts, had given her the wrong drawers and they were flipping TOP-SECRET drawers to boot.

Before she could consider this any further there came a jovial cry of 'Ahoy there teammate!' from her right and Rusty jumped in her seat as she realised that the dashing man in the following desk had peddled himself up behind. 'I'm Bartholomew Shackleton-Biscuit, but you can call me Toad. Glad to have you aboard.' He held out an elegant hand, but before she could take it her desk began to turn a corner and he disappeared out of sight. Before he reappeared again Nancy called out from just ahead,

'Beverage Row, time to grab a cuppa, just follow my lead.' Rusty realised that this whole stretch of corridor had a complicated looking dispensing facility running alongside it, festooned with buttons, dials, pipes and its own little conveyor belt that run alongside at shoulder height.

'Select your choice of cup first,' called out Nancy, clicking one of the chunky looking buttons causing a china teacup drop from a little rack and onto the mini belt. 'Then you pick your choice of beverage...' continued Nancy, but Rusty was not really listening as her desk drew level with the daunting machine and the first row of ten buttons labelled with things like Medium Mug, and Dainty Teacup confronted her.

'Er c-c-choice of cup?!' she gurgled looking anxiously at the row of buttons.

'Then dial in your strength and temperature...' continued Nancy from somewhere up ahead as the contraption started to gurgle and vent steam. The cup selection panel was now receding behind her, no choice yet having been made, and she had to reverse peddle a little to stay alongside. This is turn caused the man called Toad and the other following desks to begin have to peddle away also.

'Oh, sorry, but I don't know...I er, oh cup!' she stammered realising, as she bumped into Toad's following desk, that a choice was required without delay or she would miss out altogether. In panic she jabbed at a button labelled "Largest Flagon' and a gigantic pewter cup dropped down onto the little belt and began to chug towards the leaf dispenser section. 'Oh gosh no,' cried Rusty, almost in tears and jabbed again this time at the final button "Expresso Cupette" and a tiny porcelain cup dropped *inside* the flagon with a clunk. By now the nested cups, and a completely flustered Rusty, were drawing alongside another set of buttons, labelled for all kinds of coffees, teas and herbal concoctions, some of which she had never even heard of. 'Oh, what do I do now?!' wailed Rusty as Toad trying to be helpful leaned over her desk and gesticulated in a manly fashion.

'Select a beverage,' he suggested with a note of impatience in his tone. But it was clear that consternation was now spreading back along the track as desks started to bump into one another and much frantic reverse pedalling could be heard. 'Oh golly', he added beginning to sound alarmed, 'just select something!' Not wanting to wreck everything on her first day, Rusty closed her eyes and stabbed desperately at one of the buttons, but accidently clicked two instead and both coffee granules and a reddish looking fine leaf powder dropped into (and around) her cup stack. The next section had wheels to dial for water temperature and then levers for sugar and so forth. Utterly lost to wild panic now, Rusty whizzed and stabbed at them almost at random and sugar, water, cream and steam shot hither and thither. At this stage, however, her desk was some two feet beyond the end of the contraption, and she had to lean back over Toad's desk to try to reach her cups, which were dropping inexorably out of reach.

'Look I don't want to alarm you unduly,' started Toad, in a manner which alarmed her greatly, 'but there are points coming up and you really need to flag a direction now.' She looked ahead to see that indeed a junction in the belts was coming up and a pair of chimps were waving to try and get her attention.

'Oh goodness to buggeration, how do I, what do I?!' screamed Rusty.

Toad pointed urgently towards a little flag on a pivot at the front of her trolley. 'Flick the flag, flick the flag!' She spied the flag, but since she was now sprawled over both her and Toad's desks trying to reach her drink her only option seemed to be to reach with one pointed toe to try and flick it over. It took a good three goes, but finally her foot caught the flag flicking it to the left, and with incredible speed the two chimps pulled levers and unplugged and replugged her onto the left hand of the two tracks which headed, more or less, straight on. A little relief settled over her, but this was rather short lived as she realised with a jolt that Nancy had gone the other way and she was rapidly moving out of view into another part of the building her eyes wide in total disbelief. Toad too had signalled right, and it was too late for him to change and follow her, he raised his arms to try and calm her.

'Don't worry, it's just the meeting room branch, we'll be on the smoothway, so if you don't divert again, we should see you in the canteen. Don't do anything...' but she missed the last part as another corner meant he disappeared completely from view and Rusty was alone with her trundling desk and the sounds of the clanking from all around her. 'I didn't even get a drink,' she sobbed softly as she straightened herself up and tried to take in her surroundings.

As announced, it did indeed appear to be in a section of track with meeting rooms along one side. At each room there was a set of points and a pair of smartly dressed, if somewhat disinterested, chimps waiting to work the points and plug the telecommunication cables into the appropriate mechanisms. The rooms themselves had In and Out doors and big clocks over these to show the meeting start and end times. The corridor was very straight and clearly ran the whole length of the building and apart from a few desks at the very far end of the track, she seemed to be completely alone. Taking slow deep breaths to calm herself she had half a thought to perhaps do some work, but when she absent-mindedly opened her drawer, she was confronted again with the foreboding folder and all the panic started to rush back. She slammed the drawer shut and decided to think for much longer before making any further decisions. She flicked absent-mindedly through the rolodex wondering if perhaps she should call someone, Lost Property perhaps. But maybe the best thing was simply to ride out the day, replace the drawers and get the right ones tomorrow, and hopefully no harm done.

Just as she thought she could breathe a little easier she heard a slight commotion at the far end of the corridor. Looking up she saw one of the two mysterious men in dark coats talking loudly to the people sitting on the moving desks. Fingers were pointed tetchily, and desk drawers were being rifled, despite protests from the designers.

'Oh crikey!' yelped Rusty, 'the thugs from earlier, with the oriental girl, they must be after the TOP-SECRET plans.' It could be said that Rusty's thinking processes were now not in the best place, and quick as you like she put two and two together and came up with, well, at least six. In no time at all she managed to convince herself that these people must be foreign agents and it was now solely down to her to keep the TOP-SECRET documents out of their hands. In a near blind panic she looked down the track to see if there was a way to escape, and sure enough a meeting room junction was approaching that might do the trick. It was attended by a pair of laconic looking chimps; one of whom was dragging heavily on a pipe and watching the meeting-end clock with a modicum of attentiveness, the other seemed fast asleep. Quick as she could, without drawing undue attention to herself she clicked the little flag into what she believed was a left turn position and simultaneously waved to catch the more awake of the two ape's attention.

'Hisst,' she hissed, 'I'm going in.' The eyes nearly popped out of the primate's head as he saw this sudden change of signalling. He pointed with alarm at the meeting end clock, which was showing, very clearly to him at least, five minutes only left on the meeting.

'I know, I know, I'm late... but I am going in,' she had intended to add "whether you like it or not" but thought better of it, as she'd already upset one primate today, and this one didn't seem too thrilled by her either. The ape appeared ready to protest again but realising this was probably more than his job was worth, he shook his friend rudely awake and swung into action. In a flurry of hairy arms and legs the little ape managed to haul on the points lever, and the desk began to turn towards the slowly opening heavy wooden door. The other chimp, rather less than best pleased at being so rudely awoken, grabbed at her wiring cables and hauled them out just in time as she rattled into the ornate meeting room but alas wasn't quite quick enough to plug them into the room's cabling system before the door began to swing shut.

The area she found herself in was clearly a boardroom of some description, complete with cut glass chandelier and, horror of horrors, its own diminutive beverage dispenser. It seemed apparent that some sort of high-level meeting was just concluding and the chairwoman, in an expensive twinset and two loops of pearls, was shuffling her papers. Without looking up she announced, 'Well that's lunch I think.' With this the exit doors swung open and the six, rather more posh than usual, desks and occupants began to chug out of the room. They all stared in bemusement at the dishevelled junior draughtsperson clanking in through the entry door. 'Oh, I say, you're a smidge on the late side,' added the unsmiling chairwoman.

Rusty could only force a meek smile, half a shrug and a sighed 'Story of my day'.

The desks were now departing one by one as her's clanked and wheezed its way onto the meeting room loop. The mechanisms by the door detected the new arrival by a series of ratchets and began to spin the clocks around to new begin and end times. The last of the desks was on the threshold now and the smart young man offered a short wave at the beleaguered girl.

He glanced at his pocket watch, 'You do realise this is a two-hour meeting room?' he asked kindly. Rusty just gulped. As his desk departed through the hinged doors and Rusty's settled into its slow loop of the room he added, 'You should just make lunch though,' with a glimmer of optimism in his voice. With this the doors wheezed shut on piston-powered hinges and with a clang she was alone with the clanking rails, the balefully ticking clockworks, one TOP-SECRET folder and her madly racing mind.

Two solitary hours later after twelve circuits of the room and twelve failed attempts to get a satisfactory cup of Darjeeling (or, quite frankly, anything) from the beverage dispense-o-matic the exit door creaked open and her desk finally clanked across the points into the exit channel. Two, extremely annoyed looking, primates awaited her on the threshold, clearly not at all happy at having been required to wait for her. The most perfunctory of exit procedures was performed and no cheeky banter of any description was exchanged. Their jobs performed with the least ceremony possible they both disappeared sharpish through a small utility door to some, presumably long overdue, tea break.

Talking of tea, and indeed, breaks, Rusty's tummy gurgled emptily as the distinctive aromas of an eating facility began to waft down the corridor. Her desk clanged its way towards an open area and a clearly marked dismounting ramp. Peering out from doorway were two anxious looking visages, which Rusty was overcome with relief to realise were Nancy and Toad, glancing at their pocket watches and for their missing teammate with equal concern. She almost cried with joy and gave a little wave, which they returned in spades, clearly very happy that she'd finally turned up whilst there was still time for lunch. At this point, after the canteen dismounting point, the empty desks then reached a lift type apparatus that appeared to slowly convey them up through a hole in the ceiling to the second storey. The idea being that whilst one took luncheon one's desk moved upstairs to await the afternoon loop of the second floor. A dilemma presented itself to Rusty, should she entrust the secret documents to whatever awaited on the floor above or keep them with her? In the end, encouraged by much collegial waving to chivvy it up a bit, she decided to grab the TOP-SECRET folder and stuff it in her waistcoat. Her colleagues looked at her bemused but put it down to her being very conscientious about her work. In any case there was no time to query her actions as there was barely enough minutes to get lunch before they were due to remount their desks.

Toad offered her a welcoming hug and lead the way to the seating area. Nancy, who was not really the touchy-feely sort, shuffled on behind them.

'Gangling gadzoomers, we thought you'd been kidnapped or something!' chortled Toad.

'Or something, is p-probably right,' mumbled Rusty glancing nervously this way and that for enemy spies and potential fifth columnists.

'The canteen is over two floors,' added Nancy somewhat less emotively, 'starters and mains on this level and desserts upstairs,'

'Golly, nothing is simple in this place,' swallowed Rusty, not sure she was taking it all in. At least the food selection procedure here was a slightly less over-engineered than the drinks dispensers. They took adjoining seats at a fairly empty long table and selected starters from a simple conveyor belt of dishes (now somewhat depleted) in the centre.

'Not a lot left this time of day,' lamented Nancy, and indeed pickings were very slim, with only prawn-a-cino or "Mrs. Bubonic's™ Offal Faggots" (indicated by little labels on sticks) seemingly available. Not feeling particularly like eating, but realising she might need all her strength later, Rusty plumped for the caffeinated seafood combo as the slightly lesser of two evils and forced a cold spoonful into her mouth.

'For main course you need to look at the chalk board and then press in the number of your choice,' explained Nancy.

'Oh right,' mumbled Rusty between mouthfuls and attempted to decipher the cryptic main course descriptions set alongside 5 number codes. A handy numbered cash register type keyboard thingy was provided at each eating station for entering your choice and, being devoid of any gumption today, Rusty typed in numbers randomly until a little green ticket popped up into the selection window to indicate a choice had been accepted. She could only pray it wasn't something too awful, although with her luck today it was probably cabbage and prune omelette.

Glancing up from her prawn dish Rusty was alarmed to suddenly see the oriental looking woman enter the dining room via a side door. Trying her best to duck down behind the food carousel and disappear into the laminated tabletop and ignoring the askance looks of her companions, she glanced back to see that one of the dark clad heavies was now blocking the entrance she had used.

'Are you quite all right?' asked Nancy, with a hint of annoyance entering her voice.

'I'm, yes, well fine... oh, you know erm,' began Rusty who was now looking around for any other ways out of the dining room. The only obvious exit seemed to be the spiral staircase in the middle of the room, with a preposterously over-lit sign flashing the single word "Desserts" and a big arrow pointing upwards. 'Not sure I'm in a very erm, savoury mood, might head erm dessertwards, ish...' gibbered Rusty and gripping her chest to make sure she didn't lose the TOP-SECRET documents she got down on all fours and began to crawl under the table towards the staircase.

'But you've not even finished your prawns!' protested Toad, who hated to see food go to waste.

'Help yourself,' muttered Rusty over her shoulder, but he'd already tucked in anyway.

Halfway to the staircase there was a sudden shout and the ugly from the doorway called out, 'Hey you, on the floor, wait a minute, we need to ask you some questions.' At this point Rusty realised she couldn't really crawl all that fast, so she made a lunge for the staircase and began to clang her way frantically up the metal stairs. There were more cries from behind and the sound of footsteps running after her, but she didn't wait to find out what their line of questioning might be. With all possible haste she emerged into the dessert room, which had similar arrangements of eating areas and carousels chugging round with a selection of hot and cold puddings.

'Oh my golly gadzooks,' muttered Rusty to herself, her head spinning a little as she looked around for a way out. She could already hear boots on the stairs, so there was no time to lose and spotting the desk remounting platform made a beeline straight for it. Then without warning the other dark suited man suddenly sprang up for where he'd been seated, nibbling a cheeky chocolate meringue, and went to grab her.

'Oh no you don't!' he yelled, but before he could get hold of her, Rusty grabbed the first pudding dish she could reach and flung it at him. The man raised his arms to defend himself, but too slowly so he caught what turned out to be a steaming hot spotted dick, full in the face. There were screams and shouts from the other diners, but Rusty was on a mission now and reaching the line of desks jumped up onto the conveyor belt between the rails. Waving her arms madly, to prevent her toppling over as the belt was gaily chugging along, she began to run with it along the corridor. Behind her the first of the heavies and the oriental lady, who seemed much nimbler on her pins, appeared and, hesitantly at first, began to run down the track after her.

'Oh crikey, what *are* you doing Inglemop?' ranted Rusty to herself, but there was no going back now, she'd have to find the way out and then alert the first constable she came across, no other course of action seemed tenable.

Driven on by adrenaline, if little else, she was making such good progress along the track and around the first corner that she'd caught up with a group of four desks and had to start forcing her way past the, understandably indignant, designers at their work. A few "I say"s and "What d'yer think you're up to"s were proffered, but no one tried to impede her. There couldn't be much longer until the exit she began to think, perhaps around this next corner. However, as she turned the bend and looked down a fairly longish run of track, she realised that at the far end was the other thug! He was bent over and clearly struggling for breath, having run the whole length of the floor below to try and cut her off. She turned to go back, but hearing the other potential assailants approaching she realised she was trapped. This was a straight run of track and not a meeting room section, so she couldn't repeat her disappearing act from the floor below. Frantically she looked in all directions as the man at the far end spotted her, and despite his exhaustion (and face full of steamed pudding) began to clomp towards her. Fortunately, he made very little progress as was running against the flow of the truck, but Rusty was having to tread water now just to stay on the same spot and the two behind her were approaching very rapidly. *Oh, what to do!* There appeared to be only one option, just below where she was standing was a little door, barely a foot high. It might not even be big enough for her to get through, but the men would definitely struggle to follow her. Without hesitation and thinking only of king and country, Rusty girded her loins and made a mad dive for it. The door was not locked and opened inwards on a simple sprung hinge; she lunged through it and began to crawl frantically down a short corridor towards the sounds of chatter ahead. Hopefully, these where amenable folk who might aid her escape by showing her the quickest route outta here, she could only hope. Hearing the door behind her being rattled and yet more shouts she scrabbled manically into the room and found herself confronted by quite a scene. The room was a staff room of some description and sitting in it, enjoying a brew and a puff on a pipe or two, were a whole room of chimpanzees.

'Oh crap,' moaned Rusty as it soon became obvious that they all knew her to be the speciesist time-a-wasting chimp-botherer that they had all just been bad mouthing prior to her undignified entry. The plethora of dirty looks that were aimed in her direction cannot be adequately described by mere words alone, so I won't bother. Indeed, so bad was the level of passive aggressive enmity aimed at her that it was almost a relief when the oriental looking woman poked her head through the door behind her and offered a chirpy,

'What ho! Any chance of you holding still a while so I can arrest you?' At this request the chimps burst into spontaneous applause.

Rusty was duly arrested and bundled, mostly for her own safety, out of the chimp's staff room and post haste into the head of security's office. There the oriental looking woman revealed herself to be a King's Agent by the name of Lilly Fortitude. Her identity being duly corroborated by the Head of Security himself, Rusty burst into tears of relief and blubbed the whole sorry story of how she had come to be cornered in a tearoom full of disgruntled primates. In the end it was deemed that no real harm had been done, Fortitude and her two sidekicks took possession of the secret documents and, no further charges being deemed necessary, Rusty was let off with a stern reproach not to do such things again (she wouldn't) and an admonishment of "doncha know there's a war on," (she didn't) and released, still highly emotional, into the arms of her co-workers. They in turn put her directly onto an omnitram home with barely another word.

'Oh rats,' sighed Rusty to herself as the tram clanked and rattled her homewards, 'I totally forgot to clock out.'

And so, it came to pass that Rusty Inglemop became the shortest, or if you prefer the longest (since technically she never did end her shift) employee of the Monkey Teaspoon Design Agency. Rather than return the next day she decided instead not to see out her trial period and found a much less stressful job with a smaller company that had decidedly simpler arrangements for making hot drinks. Oh, and on the weekend, to make some small amends, she volunteered at a home for orphaned chimpanzees.

XII

Crash!

Darkness. The thin, stale air, such as it was, smelt of burnt rubber and vile oil smoke; it was also bitterly hot with a dry heat that stung the eyes and lips. There were sounds resonating in the air, the clank of cooling metal, distant shouts and cries and perhaps the urgent crackle of fire. Having barely regained consciousness a man, strapped tightly to a complicated looking chair attempted to ease his gritty eyes open and tune in any other available senses to work out where he was. He seemed unable to move his arms or legs very much and his vision was obscured by glass, perhaps a visor of some sort. His slowly waking brain tried to figure out where he was and how he might have got there. The visor was part of a cumbersome helmet attached to an equally bulky spacesuit that was weighing him down in his seat. Moving an arm cautiously to test the gravity, it seemed that it was not unusual in any way that he could detect. So most probably the craft was still on the earth rather than any extra-terrestrial location. There was a sudden grating burst of static and radio chatter in his ears, but it came and went before he could focus on it. So, he was some sort of pilot or spaceman perhaps, but he couldn't yet rule out being a diver either. The air seemed so hot he could barely breath, perhaps something was on fire or he was in a very hot place, deep underground perhaps? His limited vision began to swim; the clunky controls of the craft that he could make out began to wobble a little. There was a tremor and a rumble from somewhere distant below his feet, although he was lying on his back, it now seemed. He felt only confusion and was struggling even to recall who he was let alone what he was doing there. This absence of memory created an even odder sensation: an intense feeling of déjà vu; he'd felt this way before, possibly more than once. Although this could simply all be a trick of a damaged mind. He tried again to simply recall his own name, he was getting a letter, G perhaps or B... he rolled it on his tongue, and it seemed to have a taste, a sweet taste out of context with the bitter fumes around him. Gr, Br, Gr... he ran it round and round, it felt right, but his brain wouldn't supply any further letters. Then the stars appeared, and his head began to swim sickeningly, round and round and round and falling, falling hard. He blacked out again.

'Grenville, Grenville wake up!' the girl's voice rattled urgently in his ears, accompanied by unnecessarily violent shaking. 'Grenville, wake up, daddy says we need to go soon.'

As Grenville rolled over onto his side his lovingly crafted space helmet, actually an old kitchen colander with a pair of welding goggles on top, slipped down and pinched his ear.

'Ow!' he yelped in his juvenile tones and sat abruptly upright. He was sitting under his favourite apple tree at the bottom of his parent's garden. He remembered he'd been on the swing, in full astronaut outfit (colander helmet, old white pyjamas with lovingly sewn insignia and improvised equipment, his father's far too large old fleece-lined winter gloves sweaty on his small hands) before tiredness and warm sunlight had caused him to curl up for a nap. His twin sister, Amelia, shook him again even though he was very clearly awake now. 'Get off me!' he yelped tetchily. His sister stood with hands on the hips of her sailor dress, head cocked in a defiant posture.

'Daddy says the airship is working now, well probably, maybe. He says we have to go now; the Martians are coming.' This last statement caused the eight-year-old Grenville to come fully awake, his heart beating rapidly, his eyes staring wide. He looked back towards the house and the, faintly visible, smoke of the Metropolis beyond so see if he could spot any Martians about to devour his family home. He was only a little disappointed that no aliens were visible, but the house was a hive of frantic activity, nonetheless. The three-storey sprawling country pile that was the Lushthorpe's ancestral home was dwarfed by the imposing expanse of Papa Lushthorpe's incredible multi-tiered airship, with four main gas envelopes, quadruple steam driven propeller engines and multiple gondolas, balconies, equipment sponsons and gilded cabins. For all its incredible looming gothic beauty, its most distinctive feature was probably its lack of operation. Engineers and crew moved this way and that over the superstructure gantries, tools were waved, instruction manuals frantically leafed through and all manner of insults and instructions turned the air blue. Amongst it all the imposing sight of Papa Lushthorpe himself could be seen castigating anyone that came in his general area of influence and urging all others to greater efforts. Despite this, the airship edifice was clearly not going anywhere in a hurry. Grenville sighed to himself, and Amelia realised, with sibling satisfaction, that perhaps she had awoken him too hastily.

'I really don't think we are going anywhere just yet,' sighed Grenville.

'Don't care,' muttered Amelia as she began to stamp back towards the house, 'I'm going to finish packing with Mumsie.' Grenville watched her depart for a while, contemplating whether to go back to sleep. In the end he thought perhaps it was better to be awake and alert, just in case any Martians did make an appearance. Space General Grenville (First Class), needed to be ready for anything. So, he hauled his lanky body up off the grass and began to trudge in his heavy winter boots back towards the house.

Halfway across the lawn there came a great commotion from the airship. One of the four mighty steam engines had come suddenly to life, belching flame and steam in all obvious directions and a few surprising ones. This in turn had caused the airship to shrug off its rather pathetic moorings, and it was now chugging sedately, at a mere one or two miles per hour, down the slope away from the house towards the village church. All the ground-based attendants began a frantic attempt to re-secure it. Frenzied shouting brought all the servants and staff running from the house to assist. Grenville just yawned and continued to plod laconically towards the house. His father's crazy inventions rarely worked first time, or indeed second time, in fact often no times at all. All around the grounds were strewn the remains of previous airships, landships, boats, and all manner of other contraptions that had been abandoned in the spot where they finally gave up the ghost. It wasn't worth his effort even worrying about it, no it was far better to launch a new mission to brave the long climb (up the stairs) to Space Control, or his bedroom as his parent's insisted on calling it. He adjusted his colander on his head and brought his goggles down over his eyes. Even though he was only eight, Grenville was tall and lanky for his age and the pyjamas were a little too small, his ankles and wrists sticking out incongruously. As he came into the back door, he saw his "ray gun" on the kitchen table (it was lovingly crafted from wood and laboratory parts, and really rather looked the part). He picked it up and girded himself for the arduous adventure ahead.

Attired thus and looking really rather fearsome (he imagined), he stomped determinedly out of the kitchen into the panelled hallway. His macho demeanour was then rather broken by the nagging voice, in his head, of Mumsie commanding that he remove his boots. He contemplated ignoring this internal dialogue, since there were no adults to be seen anywhere around. But in the end, he realised his life probably wouldn't be worth living if he got mud on the rug, so he bent down to untie them.

'Grenville!' Came the urgent, but strangely subdued voice of his twin sister, who had suddenly reappeared in the corridor, her eyes wide. She continued in this odd stage whisper, 'You are not going to believe this.' Before he could ask what exactly it was that he wasn't going to believe, she told him anyway. 'There is a Martian robot in the parlour.' Oh, thought Grenville to himself, good idea, a sub mission, before the main mission, although it wasn't really like his sister to join in his space games willingly. 'No you idiot!' she continued, seeing his wry smile. 'There REALLY is a Martian robot in the parlour. A real one. From Mars! Come and see if you don't believe me.'

He didn't believe her, so clomped along behind as she trod in an exaggerated tiptoe around the corner towards the ornate oak door of the parlour. She tried to make him quiet down a bit with a stern finger to her lips as she slowly pushed the heavy door and they both peered around into the room.

Sure enough, it turned out that his daft sister was actually right. In the middle of the parlour on the second-best rug was a three-legged and extremely odd-looking six feet tall bronze robot. Curiously though, and in a weird echo of the other mad contraptions about the house, it really didn't seem to be doing anything very much. In point of fact it gave the distinct impression of being completely broken.

'Are you sure it's not one of papa's?' Whispered Grenville to his sister, reluctantly adopting her exaggerated tones of secrecy.

'No, it's not one of his, I know, for sure.'

'How do you know for sure? It looks broken like all the others.' She conceded this point with a shrug but wasn't about to change her story.

'I just know.'

'How do you just know?' growled Grenville through his teeth, getting a bit fed up with his sister's games.

'I just know...' she paused melodramatically, 'because there's a Martian in the servant's hall.' Grenville's eyes that were already at their near furthest extremes of wideness, widened to the point of maximum wideness and he gulped nervously. 'Take a look if you don't believe me,' challenged Amelia, standing back and readopting her hip hand position of which she was so fond. He gulped again.

'Fine, I will,' he said bravely and ignoring the look of alarm on her face checked his helmet was on securely and raised his ray gun.

'Actually, I was th-thinking we should probably just tell m- Mumsie,' she stuttered nervously.

'I'm Space General First Class Lushthorpe,' replied the boy dry mouthed. 'I can deal with a Martian!' In his bravado he'd almost convinced himself and before Amelia could add anything else, he stepped into the parlour and towards the looming robot. The alien contraption was still in a state of non-operation, although there was the odd spark coming from its back. The great bronze machine was nearly two foot taller than the lanky Grenville and he eased past it with great caution, his "ray gun" trained all the time on the servant's door at the back of the parlour.

'That's not a real gun you know!' whispered his sister crossly who, not wanting to be upstaged by her stupid brother, was following along behind him. He tried his best to ignore both her and the stewing butterflies in his tummy and reaching the servant's door (which was wide open) peered through. Sure enough, just as Amelia had said, there was indeed a Martian in the corridor. It was a short stubby thing, in an extremely baroque and weird looking space suit. It had its back to them and all three of its strange stalked eyes were focussed on a control box of some sort that it was currently bashing against the occasional table with what appeared to be a considerable amount of alien frustration.

'What's it doing?' muttered Grenville with extreme nervousness.

'I think its control box is broken,' whispered Amelia back as they strained to see around the door.

Finally, in a fit of extreme alien pique the Martian threw the box on the ground and turned to the door where it saw the two faces peering earnestly at it in wide-eyed terror.

'Aaaaaaaah!' they all cried in unison, and seemingly outnumbered the alien turned and fled down the corridor.

'Quick after it!' yelled Amelia.

'Really?' stuttered Grenville, feeling like he really favoured the telling Mumsie idea more at this juncture. But too late, Amelia had set off and already reached and indeed picked up the sparking and steaming control box.

'What do you think is wrong with it?' she asked, turning the dented metal box over in her hand. Before they had time to consider it further, the alien suddenly reappeared around the corridor this time with an ugly looking (and really rather enormous) laser rifle in its gauntleted hands. It's three eyes on their green protrusions staring at the children with what didn't look like it was an offer of friendship between worlds. It chuntered something though it's little sharp-toothed mouth and shortly afterwards a little grille on the front of its helmet crackled into life,

'Earth dwarves, return my robot operations box, or I shall laser you in twain!' Oddly the voice sounded rather more camp than threatening and the children didn't really know quite what to make of it.

'Now that is a real laser gun,' commented Amelia, as much to annoy her brother as anything else, although this did seem to be a salient point.

'Run?' offered Grenville. But Amelia was already gone and with a yelp Grenville dropped his pretend ray gun and ran after her.

Back they hared though the parlour and past the still immobile tri-bot the alien, in hot pursuit. 'I don't want to be lasered in twain!' complained Grenville as he caught his sister, still clutching the control box. 'Where now?'

'The laboratory,' ordered Amelia confidently, 'papa will have something there we can use, he's always banging on about weapons and things.'

'If any of them actually work,' countered Grenville morosely, but with the camp oath-chuntering alien approaching the door it seemed like the best plan. So they scarpered sharpish down the corridor, past the kitchen and into the annex. Here they found the laboratory door also wide open and, still, not a soul in sight. Between them they managed to heave the heavy door closed and threw the bolt. With their backs to the door, they could just make out the muffled clumping of the Martian and began to take in the cluttered laboratory with its workbenches, tools and chemicals laid out in chaotic fashion.

'Right, you find something to attack the Martian and I'll see if I can get the control box working,' ordered Amelia making towards a work bench to look for suitable tools. Grenville harrumphed to himself, since he was the Space General First Class, and Amelia didn't have any rank in the Olde Albion Space Command that he was aware of anyway, it seemed a bit rich for her to be issuing instructions. Still, he couldn't think of a better plan, and given that the Martian was now angrily rattling the door it was probably best to crack on. He tried to rack his brain to remember some of the "weapons and things" that papa had actually mentioned over supper and the like, but nothing much was springing to mind. In fact, the only things that seemed to be on offer were a mixture of chemicals in flasks and bottles, so he headed to look at the labels to see if any looked useful in the case of an alien invasion.

'Fixed it!' called out Amelia, with a distinct notice of triumph. Grenville looked back with a look of sarcastic disbelief on his face that his annoying sister could actually fix anything, and was about to mutter something equally sardonic to that effect. However, this ribbing of his sister would probably have to wait as without any warning a sinister orange light beam sparked menacingly though the door as the alien, done with pointless shoving, opted to laser its way into the room instead. Apart from cutting through the door the light also sliced its way through a nearby workbench, bounced off a titanium trolley and cut an arc through the ceiling. Amidst a great shower of plaster dust and steam, Grenville moved frantically to scrabble behind the chemicals' cupboard, which was also mostly metal and might afford some small shelter from the lasering-in-twain that now seemed surely inevitable. He looked back for his sister, through the settling smoke, but she and the control box were no longer at their station, he offered up a short prayer that she had also taken cover. He tried to control his breathing as the door was finally crashed off its hinges and clattered onto the floor, and he heard stomping as the alien entered the room chuntering loudly to itself. The little bronze grille sparked up again in its oddly camp yet still ominous tones.

'Earth dwarves I am flaking skin with annoyance to laser you twainwards,' it pronounced somewhat cryptically. As the stomps of the alien came cautiously closer, Grenville began to read the labels of the bottles in the cabinet with the hope of finding something useful. 'Carbolic soda, epoxy resin, distilled water, cherry punch, oh dear,' he mumbled under his breath, wishing that he'd made more effort to learn how to just read things in his head. Suddenly his mutterings were cut short as he heard his sister scream and poked his head around the cupboard, to see the alien bearing down on her and readying its rifle.

'Amelia!' he called, and the alien looked his way with two of its three eyes. Before he could think of anything else to do, with a mighty crash the great Martian tri-bot suddenly stumbled into the laboratory, thumping mightily into the door frame and nearly tumbling over. Grenville realised to his surprise that the robot was, sort of, under Amelia's control as she frantically pulled the levers and clicked the switches on the box trying to work out what each one did.

'Unhand Grogg you detached brain stem robot device of increasing annoyance!' raged the camp tones of the Martian's translation grille as it grabbed the smaller spacesuited creature and pinned its arms to its side. It seemed that Amelia was rapidly figuring out what the box did with the speed of discovery that only a child can manage, and this had bought them time to find a way to fight back. Grenville resumed his reading of labels, in the hope of finding a weapon of choice, or at the very least, last resort.

'Unhand at the large bosom of insistence your master - Grogg the mostly merciless!' ranted the alien as Grenville ran his fingers across the myriad of flasks and vessels until his eyes alighted on one that read "This does something good, but I can't remember what".

'That'll do,' muttered Grenville more in resignation than anything else and picked up the hand sized flask containing a disgusting looking brownish liquid. The alien was still in the grip of the tribot but seemed to be slowly forcing the arms apart in order to escape. Without waiting for more pronouncements Grenville hurled the flask at the glass dome of the alien and it smashed across it, releasing a sickly brown gas that quickly expanded to fill the whole laboratory.

'A puny attempt at pacification earth dwarf' mocked the translation grille in its odd tones.

'It's got a spacesuit on you idiot, that's not going to work!' shouted Amelia from the other side of the room. Oh, thought Grenville deeply annoyed that his sister was probably right. However, it seemed that perhaps the Martian's suit was actually taking in some of the atmosphere, as the brown gas seemed to be getting into the helmet.

'Grogg is not scared by your brown emanation,' started the alien grille, before adding 'I do feel rather tired though, night all.' Followed by a loud snoring noise as the alien gave every appearance of having fallen into an instant and deep sleep. Having taken great lungfuls of the brown gas themselves, Amelia and Grenville looked at each other blankly, not feeling particularly sleepy themselves. However, for the life of them, they couldn't remember how they had come to be in the laboratory and quite what was going on.

There was a great commotion from outside the laboratory and a clearly distressed papa Lushthorpe suddenly crashed into the room accompanied by two flintlock-armed servants. He took in the whole room scene, the snoring alien lovingly in the arms of its robot, the last few wisps of the pretty much dissipated brown gas and the two staring wide-eyed children.

'Children, are you harmed?' he enquired through heaving breaths.

'I'm fine papa,' muttered Amelia and Grenville nodded too as his father glanced between them both.

'What in god's name has happened here?' spluttered papa.

'This alien's in some sort of coma,' came another voice that the children did not recognise.

'I don't know papa,' muttered Grenville looking very shocked himself, 'how did we even get in here, what are those things? I feel weird!' And he truly did, not so much through sickness but more a deeply unsettling feeling that he really didn't understand how he came to be in this situation. The last thing he could remember was going to bed, supposedly the previous night, and now he was in his father's laboratory amongst wreckage, aliens, robots and staring wide-eyed adults. He saw stars and his vision started to swim alarmingly. Then he fainted cold out.

'Grenville, Grenville.' There was a voice from somewhere, muffled and indistinct accompanied by a shaking vibration. He realised his eyes were gummed shut and he was struggling to open them. It was also unbearably hot and grimy sweat was running down his face. He had no idea where he was or what was happening.

'Sir Lushthorpe, we need to get you out, the rocket is on fire!' The voice was of an earnest sounding young woman. He managed to ply one eye reluctantly open and stared towards the sound through a glass visor of some sort. Sure enough it was indeed a young woman in a space suit with the helmet removed, she was tugging at his straps where they attached to some sort of complicated looking seat.

'Amelia?' he garbled through dry lips.

'No Sir,' replied the young lady sounding confused, 'It's Ellen, are you all right? We need to get you out urgently.' Memories started to drift back to him. The weird feeling of déjà vu persisted though.

'Ellen, thank god. Yes, help me up.' He began to use his arms to help him extricate himself from the chair.

'Are you hurt?'

'Nothing that won't mend,' he muttered pushing up the helmet visor so he could see more clearly the wreckage of mangled machinery around him. He shook his head, but the déjà vu just wouldn't shift. 'I've had the strangest dream though.' And with that more arms, and a cat, arrived and assisted Ellen in removing Sir Grenville Lushthorpe from his gigantic crashed rocket to safety.

To be continued...

XIII

The War Cabinet Meets

<u>THE CAST IN ORDER OF APPEARANCE</u>

Horsen Cart – An Actor

Igor Beaver – ARC World Service Reporter

An Unnamed Waiter

First Lord of the Admiralty Cuthbert

Air Chief Marshal Fairey Loveboat

Sir Arthur Coward – Homeland Defence (and Attack) Secretary

Mrs. Hildenbrand-Fogg – Cabinet Secretary

Mrs. Tickle III (Feline)

Tobias Fitch – Hired Gun

The Prime Minister

Hieronymus Gunquit – Private Secretary to the PM

Sir Grenville Lushthorpe - Inventor

Scarlett Carshalton – The King's Astronomer (Nut)

Admiral Sherman (Canine)

An Unnamed Police Constable

SCENE 1

INTERIOR: MUSTY A.R.C. RADIO STUDIO

CART:

Indulge me if you will as I take you back to the dark days of the 2nd Great Martian War. A time when hope still lived in human hearts (but only just) and the mighty Martian war machine had been halted by oak-hearted yeomanry long abandoned on the Moon (but only for a while). At this time of great peril, the Prime Minister moved the king and government to a secret location on the south coast of Albion. There deep within the white cliffs he called together his war cabinet and drew up his plans to crush the alien invaders and send help most soonest, if not sooner, to our brave boys in space.

This drama, created by the legendary playwright Estevez Vortex Pyjamas is based on true events around that troubled time and, although it takes some dramatic licence, is a faithful portrayal of how the seeds for the vanquishing of man's foes were planted.

Ladies and gentlemen, do not be alarmed by the realistic nature of this performance, for these events are in the past. Nevertheless, we should always be vigilant: as we can never be sure when the red menace might return once more. So, look to the stars and remain resolute.

And enjoy this play, which is entitled: The War Cabinet Meets.

SCENE 2

INTERIOR: BUSY MID-PRICE RESTAURANT CORRIDOR

OVERLY DRAMATIC ORCHESTRA PLAYS

BEAVER: This is New Albion calling, New Albion calling, this is
       Igor Beaver on behalf of the ARC World Service. We
       interrupt this programme of mediocre parlour music to
       take you to momentous events happening this very
       evening. I'm currently standing in a secret location in
       the south of Albion.

WAITER: It's not all zat secret.

BEAVER: Sorry sir, what's that you say?

WAITER: Zis is Pierre's Bistro in ze 'Igh Cliffs Tea Rooms.

BEAVER: Well I'm told it's meant to be a secret, so perhaps we
       shouldn't mention it. Can I ask who are you sir?

WAITER: I am your waiter for ze evening, would you like to order
       any drinks?

BEAVER: No! I'm trying to work, but thank you.

       I'm sorry about that ladies and gentlemen. As I said, I
       am standing in a secret location awaiting the arrival of
       the PM and his war cabinet. In fact, I think I hear them
       coming now. Yes indeed, here is First Lord of the
       Admiralty Cuthbert and Air Chief Marshal Fairey
       Loveboat let's see if we can listen in.

CUTHBERT: Well what I don't bally understand is why we are banged up here in Pierre's Bistro, grotty old hole. If we were going to countermand any restaurant, why didn't we get the Brasserie!

LOVEBOAT: Oh, the King called bagsys on that one old thing!

CUTHERT: Did he indeed, snooty little brat, I never liked him much.

LOVEBOAT: Too right old boy, put the PM's nose right out of joint.

CUTHBERT: (GUFFAWS) Well that's almost made up for it.

BEAVER: Well Ladies and Gentlemen I hope you got some of that, we are in such a privileged position to hear these great statespeople discussing affairs at this momentous time for your country. Wait I can hear some more people approaching, I can see Sir Arthur Coward Homeland Defence (and Attack) Secretary and Scarlett Carshalton the King's Astronomer. Lady, gentleman a word for our listeners?

CARSHALTON: Well this Martian carry-on has certainly put a spanner amongst the pigeons!

BEAVER: Thank you Miss Carshalton, erm profound as always. Now who's this, I do believe it's Mrs. Hildenbrand-Fogg the newly appointed Cabinet Secretary, and another man I don't recognise, but what's that she's holding, it looks like some sort of animal. Yes, yes, it looks like a cat to me, who's the cat Mrs H-F?

FITCH: Mrs Tickle the Third, now out of the way!

BEAVER: (GULPS) Sorry. That voice was the mystery man, and what a brute he looks. They've gone in now, but here are the last few people. I can recognise a few, Sir Grenville Lushthorpe the crackpot inventor...

LUSHTHORPE: I beg your pudding?

WAITER: A little early for ze dessert menu monsieur, but if you insist.

BEAVER: No time for that, here comes the PM himself, with his private secretary. Let's listen in again.

PM: (MUTTERING TO HIMSELF) Bloody King, taking the bloody Brasserie, like he runs the country or something...

GUNQUIT: Yes, Prime Minister.

BEAVER: Well that looks like everyone, time to head inside. No wait who's this, it's a ruddy looking police constable and a very shaggy dog, I'm guessing some kind of security detail.

CONSTABLE: Oh ho, no, no, no, this is Admiral Sherman, she's here to represent the police force. Ho, ho, ho. Any chance of a cup of tea?

WAITER: Certainly monsieur, camomile or Earl Grey? Perhaps something for le chien?

CONSTABLE: Ho, ho, ho, just a cuppa regular, thank you very much. Who's Lucian by the way?

BEAVER: Well I've seen it all now, cats, dogs, and half the nutters in the kingdom. Well it looks like the cabinet meeting is about to start, so I'd better head inside. Stay tuned New Albion, I'll be back shortly.

DRAMATIC ORCHESTRA STABS

SCENE 3

INTERIOR: MID-PRICE RESTAURANT DINING ROOM, NOISES OF CHATTER

BEAVER: I'm talking to you now in hushed tones as we have been granted unheard of privileged access to the emergency Cabinet Room itself. Everyone seems to be in place, and yes, the Prime Minister is standing up. Here we go folks.

PM: (CLEARS THROAT MELODRAMATICALLY) Ladies, Gentlemen if you would please come to order.

NOISES CONTINUE

Ladies, er Gentlemen, please I would like to begin this cabinet meeting.

NOISES CONTINUE UNABATED BY THE PM'S PATHETIC ADMONISHMENTS

SHERMAN: (LOUD BARK)

CUTHBERT: (STARTLED OUT OF HIS AMPLE SKIN) Oh, how's your father!

PM: Goodness. Yes, well thank you Admiral Sherman. If I may get started.

(CLEARS THROAT AGAIN, HOWEVER THIS TIME OSTENTATIOSLY)

Ladies and Gentlemen, I have called you all here to this secret location...

WAITER: It's really not all zat secret, it's Pierre's... (INTERUPTED)

CARSHALTON: Shhhh!

PM: ...in very grave and dangerous times for New Albion. As you know the Martian peril has returned again and it is our...

WAITER: Can I take zome drinks orders first?

PM: Do you mind, I'm trying to address the war cabinet!

CUTHBERT: Can I see the wine list?

PM: Cuthbert, please. As I was saying, this is a grave and dangerous time.

WAITER: Perhaps zome bread for ze table?

PM: No, no bread for anyone!

WAITER: Olives zen?

PM: No blasted olives either, may I please get on. Who the devil are you anyway?

WAITER: I am your waiter for zis evening. Perhaps I should just take your starters?

PM: Starters?

SHERMAN: (BARK)

PM: What now?

CONSTABLE: (GAZING KEENLY AT THE MENU) Oh, ho, ho. The Admiral would like the meat sharing platter.

CUTHBERT: Bally good idea!

CONSTABLE: Just for herself mind.

CUTHBERT: Well quite, I'll have two of those...

CARSHALTON: Can I get two mains as a starter?

PM: Desist! No starters! No drinks! No bloody olives! This is the is the war cabinet for heaven's sake.

               Away, away with you!

WAITER: Well I'm only trying to 'elp. I'll be just 'ere if you need anyzing.

PM: I don't need any zing, I mean thing.

SHERMAN: (GROWLING)

PM: (SIGHING) What is it now?

CONSTABLE: Oh, oh. Is that, is that... oh I hardly dare say it! Oh, the horror!

PM: Spit it out man!

CONSTABLE: Is that...

PM: Yes?

CONSTABLE: Is, that, can that possibly be... A CAT?

SHERMAN:	(MUCH GROWLING)
H-FOGG:	This is not just any old cat
FITCH:	Yeah, that's Mrs Tickle the third, she risked her life to bring us a message from the moon.
SHERMAN:	(GROWL EXPRESSING CONFUSION)
CONSTABLE:	Oh ho, right, now I've heard it all!
PM:	Enough! Enough! Oh, I'm losing the will to live. (COUGHING) Waiter, some water please.
WAITER:	Zertainly sir, still or sparkling?
PM:	Neither, just a bally glass of tap water! What's the matter with everyone today? (COUGHING) Mrs H-F help me out!
H-FOGG:	Certainly Horace. If everyone could just settle down a little.
	Thank you. Now Mrs Tickle the Third risked her furry little body to bring us an important message from the Albion Defence Forces on the Moon. Even now, they are putting up a stout resistance to the Martian hordes... but they cannot hold out for long.
LUSHTHORPE:	Quite, quite! So, if I may interrupt, we need a way to get to the Moon and relieve them!
H-FOGG:	Most certainly, thank you Sir Grenville.
CUTHBERT:	But how is the question?

LOVEBOAT: Well we in the air force have some jolly big airships, surely we can load one up and rise to the occasion, as it were. It's straight up after all, hardly a problem. Be there in a jiffy.

CARSHALTON: Nincom-ninny-banana!

LOVEBOAT: I beg your pardon?

CARSHALTON: It's nothing, nothing I tell you.

LOVEBOAT: Well why are you interrupting then?

LUSHTHORPE: The good lady astronomer means it's the cold vacuum of space. Airships really only work in, erm air. Bit of a clue in the name.

LOVEBOAT: Really, no one told me.

PM: Look this really can't be that hard, how did they get up there in the first place?

DEAFENING SILENCE

Eh, anyone, someone must know? Honestly, I know it was fifty years ago, but it's like there some sort of collective amnesia.

LUSHTHORPE: Collective amnesia you say... well that doesn't ring a bell. Whatever the reason, what matters is that we have a solution now, and I do! Well sort of.

PM: Splendid work, out with it man.

LUSHTHORPE: I've built... A ROCKET!

GENERAL NOISES OF ACCLAMATION AT THE NEWS OF LUSHTHORPE'S ROCKET

PM: Good man, I knew you'd have a solution.

LOVEBOAT: Sorry to butt in, but that's Air Force territory, wot wot, Eh? I demand we take control immediately.

LUSTHORPE: Well it's not been tested yet.

LOVEBOAT: No problem. Hand it over!

LUSHTHORPE: Also, it's probably a bit underpowered and unlikely to clear earth's atmosphere. In fact, now I think about it, it's liable to crash in a fearsome fireball in some remote and unknowable location on the globe.

LOVEBOAT: Oh right, right. You're on your own then.

PM: Gentlemen, if I may. So we do have a rocket, but it's unable to acquire the necessary momentum to reach the Moon? Mmm, well it's a start. Anyone got any ideas? (A BIT DESPERATE) Anyone at all?

WAITER: About zis rocket?

PM: No salad! We're trying to think.

WAITER: Not zat rocket, zis rocket, ze one you are whiffling on about.

PM: Oh right, that one. What about it?

WAITER: Could you launch it from untran?

PM:	Untran? What, what, what's that? Translate someone please.
SHERMAN:	(BARKS TRANSLATION)
CONSTABLE:	Oh, ho, ho. The Admiral says he means "a train".
PM:	A train, well why didn't he say so.
WAITER:	Oui, un train, as I zed. My brother, 'e works on ze Tri-Transcontinental Zexpress, it' is ze fastest train on ze planet.
PM:	Zexpress?
LUSHTHORPE:	He means the Tri-Transcontinental Express, it's certainly a thought, mount the rocket on the train, get it up to speed and launch! It might just work.
CUTHBERT:	Only one way to find out!
CARSHALTON:	It's a dirty job, but someone's got to flush it.
CUTHBERT:	Glad that's sorted, waiter!
WAITER:	Oui qui?
CUTHBERT:	No, I'm fine, but thank you for your concern. Can I get the steak?
CARSHALTON:	Can I get two desserts as a main?
LOVEBOAT:	All of the above I think, plus Champagne all round, tally ho! Wot, wot.
SHERMAN:	(WOOF)

MRS TICKLE: (MIAOW)

PM: Oh for heaven's sake.

GENERAL NOISES OF CELEBRATION: BARKING, RHUBARB ETC

BEAVER: And there you have it ladies and gentlemen. The first war cabinet meeting is drawing to a close. Plans are afoot to head to Gaul across the Channel and strap a rocket to a train. What can possibly go wrong? And so, to the Moon! This is Igor Beaver for the ARC World Service signing off.

SCENE 4

INTERIOR: STILL MUSTY A.R.C. RADIO STUDIO

CART: And so, it was decided, and the first war cabinet meeting drew to a close with plans afoot to head to Gaul, across the Channel, and strap a rocket to a train. What can possibly go wrong?

BEAVER: Hey, I just said all that.

CART: Clear orf, I'm not paying you any extra for this you know.

And so, to the Moon!

DRAMATIC AND EXPENSIVE SOUNDING ORCHESTRAL MUSIC

BEAVER: Pompous twit.

CART: Bloody yank.

THE END

XIV

Admiral Sherman Solves Another Case

or The Mystery of the Missing Missive

'How's ee yer uncle Betty!' cried the nearest fielder as half the team of the Metropolis Irregular Third XI jumped in the air with fervent abandon. The hound - Admiral Sherman - and her erstwhile companion Dr Wattsat leaned a little further forward in their respective pews to see what the umpires' decision in this, clearly borderline, leg before might be.

'Typical,' sighed Wattsat, 'now they're all appealing, but that was clearly creeping down leg-side.' The Admiral was forced to agree with this statement before lapping noisily at her bowl of Baskerville Stout.

'What is creeping down who's leg?' enquired a newcomer to the group, sidling her way down the row to approach the sleuthing duo. The Admiral turned with annoyance to shush the arrivee only to see that it was none other than the robust frame of The Right Honourable Eva Blazer the New Albion *Minister of Particularly Ticklish Foreign Affairs* and, dragging her hairy frame up onto her hind legs, nudged her companion to make space for her to sit. 'I'll be honest with you,' she continued, 'I really don't follow the rules of Quad Cricket.'

'Oh, it's not so difficult,' began the doctor, shuffling across to make room, 'There are four teams, two batting and two bowling on two wickets set at right angles to each other, like a cross. Ah the japes as the runners attempt to avoid each other. Mind you there was controversy last year when they replaced the coin toss with a day of speed chess...' His voice tailed off as the Right Honourable Lady seemed not particularly inclined to follow his explanation and then raised a hand to halt him completely.

'Another time perhaps,' she chided, 'I have rather more important matters to discuss, if I may.'

'Well if you are looking for a detective to solve a case, I'm afraid the Regina and I have retired.' As if to emphasis the point, he leaned back in his pew and made a not very discrete effort to earwig the outcome of the recently heard appeal.

'I'm aware of this, but the matter in hand is rather, well ticklish. And could be extremely troublesome to one of our leading allies. There are very few agencies with sufficient clearance...' The good lady was interrupted this time by loud sigh from the sparse crowd around them, as it seemed that the result of the appeal had been "not out", and to cap it all the Antipodean All Stars had sneaked three additional runs in the hiatus.

'Ah, we're going to be flat last in this game,' moaned the good doctor slapping his thigh in frustration. 'Just typical!'

'Please if I may have your attention for just a few minutes, I'm sure you'll be interested in helping me out. Well, not just me, but the whole country.'

'Very well madam,' the doctor turned back to her, 'how can we be of assistance?'

'Well it's all rather embarrassing,' began the lady minister in subdued tones, 'but somehow a very compromising letter has gone missing from my state box. The nature of the letter is so sensitive that if the contents of it were revealed then the consequences could be catastrophic. That it could lead to war is not an idle understatement.'

Well by now she had their attention and not even synchronous sixes by both the Antipodeans and the Caledonian Chairman's XI could tear their interest back to the field. In any case it seemed the game was lost to the New Albionions, with a very real possibility of fourth place in this particular game. So, with no great reluctance, they retired from the match to the relative cool of the Metropolitan Quad Cricket Club member's bar to chew over the juicier details of this delicious sounding mystery.

And so it was that, glass in hand, the minister explained to them that the compromising letter, had indeed gone missing from her official red box two nights before. But the nature of it was so potentially embarrassing and indeed, confidential, that only the PM and the minister knew of its location and it was impossible to conceive how anyone even knew it was there to be purloined in the first place.

Admiral Sherman chewed thoughtfully on a handful of pork scratchings in contemplation, however the good doctor, who was getting a little tipsy on his third pint of porter, had an immediate theory.

'Wait a minute, aren't we missing the obvious?' Clearly not that obvious, as both the hound and the minister looked at him blankly. 'It's like that story, you know the detective one, Sheerluck Hums, or something? No? I read it only last Fall, it turned out that the minister's wife had been having an affair and been blackmailed, due to the same, to remove the letter by foreign powers, her not knowing what it's true contents were, naturally.'

'I hope you are not suggesting my husband is having an affair?' exclaimed the minister looking really rather unamused at the suggestion.

'Well now, can your rule it out?' accused Dr Wattsat brandishing his pipe in an accusatory fashion.

'He's been dead a year!' responded the minister not best pleased. This in turn caused the Admiral to spit out her mouthful of ale and bury her head in her large paws.

'Oh, right, sorry your worship. Not that then, not that at all,' feeling rather flustered, the doctor thought it was best at this point to shut his cakehole lest further inflammatory theories emerged unbidden.

The minister took a deep breath to calm herself and let out a slight sigh. 'Although, now you mention him, the butler swears he thinks the house is haunted. We'd only moved in a couple of months before my husband's untimely passing.'

Well by this point the Admiral had heard all she needed to. A missing diplomatically important missive, a possible haunting, it sounded just the thing to break the tedium of retirement, Quad Cricket notwithstanding. She let out a loud affirmative bark which caused everyone present to jump in their lounge chairs. After they had regained their composure it was confirmed that the Admiral would take the case and with much smug satisfaction, yet another round of drinks was ordered to celebrate.

Two days later the Admiral and Dr Wattsat arrived at the country pile of the minister to begin their investigations. In the interregnum it seemed that more spooky goings-on had occurred, and the butler had quite a catalogue of weirdness to report. Items had gone missing or been mysteriously moved about the place. Nothing of such consequence as the missing letter, but inconvenient all the same. Even the house itself in a secluded part of the Old Forest seemed mysterious and, more than a little creepy.

'And all these strange happenings appear to only occur after dark?' enquired the doctor sucking thoughtfully on his pipe, whilst the Admiral sniffed noisily around the minister's distinctly quirky office, festooned as it was with odd-looking pipes, mechanisms and wires, in the eastern range of the house. The butler nodded his agreement to the statement. 'Then there is no alternative, we'll have to stay over and see what happens this evening.' He bent over to examine a very bizarre clock-type-thing with a weird array of dials and buttons, built into the wall only a couple of foot off the floor. 'Distinctly weird office this, case in point: what's this clock all about then?' Muttered the doctor tapping the offending instrument with his pipe stem, the doing of which caused a series of ominous rumblings and clankings to emit from the wall and the floor all around them.

'Please don't do that!' muttered the minister, looking a tad annoyed. The doctor looked more than a little shaken, and he seemed to be re-appraising his bold statement to reside the night in this, clearly, haunted house. 'Well in any case, about the staying over thing,' continued the lady minister looking a tad uncomfortable. 'I'm afraid there is a slight problem there.'

'It's not really up to me, the Admiral must observe comings and goings for herself, she can't solve your case without all of the relevant facts,' admonished the doctor in a mildly patronising way.

'Quite, quite, well it's not that you *can't* stay here it's more that you'll need this.' With a swish of her hand the butler was dismissed from the room and returned mere seconds later holding, at arm's length - with a pair of tongs - what appeared to be the skinned pelt of a rather large, and manky cat.

'And what is *that* exactly?' enquired the doctor somewhat alarmed as the Admiral raised one hairy eyebrow in extreme scepticism.

'Well this is what the young folk like to call a cat onesie, or some such,' declared the minister.

'A cat onesie, what pray do you intend us to do with that?'

'Well I'm afraid the Admiral is going to have to wear it.' With this terrible suggestion the Admiral's eyes nearly bulged out of her skull. Seeing that they were clearly none the wiser, the minister continued undaunted. 'My elderly father is staying with us tonight, Major Blazer, and since the unfortunate incident in the Congo he's developed a bit of a phobia of canines.'

'So, are you saying that she has to wear this, this... outfit?'

'Well indeed, what's wrong with that?'

'Well it's a cat suit for heaven's sake! And the Admiral is a five-foot-long, three feet high bitch. I really don't think anyone will be fooled by this pathetic attempt at a disguise. Don't you have a bearskin or a rhinoceros suit or something a smidge less, erm offensive?'

'Well I'm awfully sorry, but it's all I've got and I'm afraid I must insist. It's for your own good after all, what happened to the last dog that came in contact with my father, I really don't wish to relay.'

'Oh, for heaven's sake!' exclaimed the doctor, again, but it seemed there was to be no argument in the matter.

And so it came to pass that a few hours later, the Admiral slinked back into the study looking rather sheepish in her terrible "cat" disguise. The butler had arranged an occasional bed for the doctor and to complete the "deception", an over-sized cat basket for the Admiral. Seeing their discomfort at both the outfit and, in the doctor's case, the possible encounters with ghouls to come the butler tried to make a little small talk.

'You know my mother thought her house was haunted.'

'Oh really,' replied the doctor who couldn't have sounded less interested if he'd tried really, really hard.

'Yes, turned out to be a false alarm.'

'Really, what was it then.'

'Squirrels in the attic.' The Admiral and the doctor exchanged sceptical glances.

'Squirrels in the attic you say?'

'Yes, it was the nuts that gave them away in the end.' By this point the sleuths two were trying their best to ignore him as they made up their beds and prepared to settle in for the night.

'Talking of nuts,' continued the butler, without being asked. 'The last owner of this house was a bit of an eccentric.'

'I'd have never of guessed,' sighed the doctor adjusting his night cap and glancing around the bizarre room. However, a nudge from the Admiral, who seemed more interested in this titbit caused him to add a supplementary, 'er well who was that then?'

'A so-called inventor, Clatterbang was his name I think.' With this revelation, a glimpse of a smile crossed the Admiral's face, before she remembered she was dressed up as a mangy cat, and her face fell again. Nevertheless, she headed off around the room sniffing eagerly at the skirting board again. After a while she returned to the good doctor and pawed keenly at his leg.

'Ah, what's that Admiral? Oh right. Yes, okay then. Er, my good man,' started Wattsat turning to the butler. 'The Admiral would like to use your telegrammatic equipment if that is acceptable at this late hour.' The butler eyed the hound carefully, before replying, with only a certain degree of scepticism.

'Well as long as she doesn't come across the major in the hall, she can help herself. It's the third door on...' his voice tailed off, as The Admiral, needing no directions to locate the necessary equipment from a mere butler, hustled busily out of the room. 'Not fooling anyone that outfit,' muttered the butler as he extinguished the gas lamp and left the doctor on his own in the spooky room with just a flickering candle for company.

Maybe two, maybe three hours later the doctor was still wide awake and fidgeting nervously with his woollen blankets. Prepared at any second to haul them over his eyes should any apparition appear. In truth the room had been fairly quiet since the Admiral's return and, despite the itchy "cat" outfit she was still required to wear, she had slept soundly since then, without so much as a murmur.

It was probably getting on for three oh the clock when a sudden ticking and clicking noise from somewhere near the strange timepiece on the wall caused the doctor's hackles to rise sharply.

'Oh my goodness,' muttered the good doctor under his breath, 'what strange ghouls are awakening?' he whimpered further. Were those just clanking pipes he could hear or the rattling chains of hell? His mind was racing with fearsome imagery, but the Admiral did not stir. Then as no further noises came the doctor was just about to relax when out of the corner of his eye, he noticed with rising alarm, a piece of paper was making its way steadily across the floor. No obvious mechanism could be seen in the flickering half-light and the doctor was beginning to convince himself it was just being moved by a breeze from the fireplace, when it made a sharp right turn and continued in a dead straight line, right past the Admiral's quietly snuffling nose. This was more than the doctor could take, with a loud cry of anguish he threw himself from the bed and raced in a mad panic from the room.

'Ghouls! Ghosts! Haunted paper!' he screamed, waking all and sundry with his mad yelling. Very much shaken and indeed stirred the butler and the lady minister (still in her dressing gown) rushed to find out the source of the hullabaloo. Thankfully, for the Admiral at least, Major Blazer did not awaken.

When they had all finally arrived back at the study, and The Admiral been roused with much shaking, it was found that the paper had mysteriously vanished, and no further evidence of paranormal activity could be detected. The Admiral seemed entirely nonplussed and after a terse discussion it was agreed that the Admiral would maintain the vigil, whilst the doctor would be allowed to sleep in the guest bedroom. It was deemed to be for the best but, still more than a little perturbed, the doctor did not manage a great deal of sleep.

The next day, following a hearty breakfast, the motley crew were summoned by The Admiral to return to the scene of the crime and it seemed a reasonable assumption that the solution to mystery was about to be revealed. Dr Wattsat, somewhat tired, but glad that he had survived the night unmolested by further satanic stationary, recounted his nighttime encounter to the Admiral in great detail whilst they awaited the arrival of the others. As she pretended to listen a slight smirk spread across her hairy muzzle.

'I don't know what you're grinning about,' muttered the doctor as he concluded his tale, 'you're still dressed as an oversized stuffed cat y'know.' And he was indeed right. But this was just as well as first to arrive was the Lady *Minister of Particularly Ticklish Foreign Affairs* wheeling her elderly father – the dreaded major – in a rickety metal wheelchair before her.

'Who are all of you!' he yelled fearsomely, brandishing his stick and gazing at each in turn with his one good eye. He seemed ready to offer further inquisition until said eye fell upon the Admiral trying to make herself look as small and cat like as possible in her terrible feline costume. 'Oh,' he muttered, a note of joviality entering his tone, 'who's that lovely pussy? Here pussy, pussy.' The Admirals eyes went as wide as anyone had ever seen, but further embarrassment was spared by the noisy entry of the butler clearing his throat in a melodramatic manner.

'It seems the Admiral has a visitor,' he announced sceptically, but before anyone could enquire further an eccentric character in tails, top hat and clockwork monocle came striding into the study.

'Professor Clatterbang at your service,' he pre-empted the gawping mouthed butler, 'Got your message Admiral, hope I'm not too late! Nice to be back in the old homestead, much missed, much missed!' Relieved to have a bigger distraction in the room than herself the Admiral's eyes returned to their usual wideness and she raised one eyebrow to the Professor.

'Professor?' interrupted the lady minister, 'to what do we owe this great pleasure?' She glanced anxiously from the professor to the dog and then back again. '*You* haven't stolen the missing letter, have you?'

'Stolen, letter!' exclaimed the professor, 'I really wouldn't think so.'

'Then why are you here?' the lady minister was beginning to lose patience with the day's proceedings.

'Ah,' stepped in Dr Wattsat, as the proverbial penny was beginning its descent. 'I expect the professor is here as he is in some way able to explain the missing missive. Isn't that right Admiral?' The dog/cat hybrid appeared fairly pleased with this observation and as everyone watched, and the major drooled slightly, she made her way first to the strange timepiece on the wall and then to some odd holes set low in the skirting board in the corner of the room. She sniffed loudly and then looked towards the professor.

'What's that, you think my mechanism has something to do with your "mystery"? Ah wait, missing letter you say.' The minister and the Admiral nodded enthusiastically in agreement. 'Ah, y'know I'd quite forgotten about this, but now you've reminded me, I expect you'd like a little demonstration.' Before anyone could enquire further as to what the Pilkington-Rhubarb he was on about, he looked around for a prop and seized, without really thinking about it, the first bit of paper he could see on the nearby desk and crumpled it up into a ball.

'Now look here!' exclaimed the lady minister taking her turn to be wide-eyed, 'those are important state papers!' He ignored her completely and throwing the paper on the floor moved over to the odd-looking clock in the wall.

'Now then, I see you've wound up my TTT timing mechanism,' he said, presumably to the butler, whilst squinting to take in the position of the clock hands and settings of the dials.

'Timing mechanism?' asked the doctor, becoming increasingly interested and wondering if he should start to take some notes.

'Yes, yes,' he squinted again, 'Timing mechanism indeed.' And with that he reached out one bony finger and whizzed the minute hand around until he heard a click and a slight bong.

'That's the noise from last night!' exclaimed Dr Wattsat. But his statement of the obvious was cut mercifully short as without warning a small portion of the skirting board shuffled upwards and from various little holes around the room tiny robots whizzed out and across the floor. As all those present watched they quickly scooted over the shag pile until the first one found the crumpled paper. Then with incredible efficiency they all converged and seized the paper with tiny pincers and moved in a dead straight line back towards the hole in the skirting board where they promptly disappeared: paper, robots and all. The professor clapped his hands with glee.

'Ah they still work, one of my finest inventions, I'd quite forgotten.' At this point the doctor glanced wryly at the Admiral who was looking really rather pleased with herself. 'TTT. Teeny Tiny Tidybots!' exclaimed the professor who was now foaming slightly at the mouth. 'Meant to tell you! Honest. Too complicated to move, but if you wind the mechanism up, you've only yourself to blame.'

'So,' interrupted the lady minister, holding up her hand to silence the bonkers inventor. 'Are you telling me that your tiny robot housemaids have dumped my internationally sensitive correspondence in the garbage?' She sounded not at all thrilled by the possibility.

With this accusation the Admiral, still encumbered by her terribly ill-fitting cat suit, trotted over to where a series of letter-sized alcoves were set in the wall near the desk. She sniffed furiously amongst the filed missives and then gently pulled out a single letter from one of the slots with her teeth. She trotted over to the lady minister who carefully took the envelope from her mouth and glanced over it urgently. A relieved smile spread over her face and it seemed the letter had been found.

'Not in the bin, oh dearie me no. Filed y'know. I'm not a philistine. What did you think those pigeonholes were for anyway?' muttered the professor to no one in particular. All eyes by this point, were on the Admiral, who it seemed had solved another case with aplomb.

'Well done Admiral,' congratulated the lady minister, and all present nodded their respect, with the exception of the major who, attempting to wheel his rickety wheelchair towards the hound muttered only,

'Here beautiful pussy come to the major, so I can tickle your ears!'

With this the Admiral left the room as though someone had set fire to her tail with the major wheeling frantically in hot pursuit.

'Well, that's wrapped that up nicely,' boomed Dr Wattsat, 'Another case solved. What to do with the rest of the day? Anyone fancy catching a spot of Quad Cricket?' He glanced around the ensemble hopefully, but it seemed that all of a sudden everyone had something really rather important to do and one after the other they made their excuses and left.

'Typical,' muttered the good doctor, 'just typical.' And, indeed, it very much was.

XV

Crash Again!

Things had not been going particularly well since Ellen Hall had safely landed the great four-winged Sultan's Star Super Transport next to the giant triple-train mounted moon rocket, that was Sir Grenville Lushthorpe's latest manifestation. The issue was not the gigantic rocket itself, which seemed in fine fettle, poised as it was, on the centre of three great steam locomotives preparing to haul it to take-off speed. No, that was all hunky dory. As was the company of marines now dismounting from the Super Transport with only a mild case of air sickness. Even her erstwhile brother-in-arms, the alien plasma rifle and space cat toting mercenary – Tobias Fitch – had survived more or less intact, given that he was not particularly keen on flying (for historical reasons). No indeed that was all just as it should be, the real problem seemed to be with head of the air force, and New Albion's foremost test pilot – Air Commodore Fairey Loveboat's rumbling stomach. Barely had the passenger doors been opened on the many piston-engined plane before he had marched up to the nearest orderly and demanded to know 'What time's lunch old boy, wot wot?' Notwithstanding the fact that the orderly was, in point of truth, a rather fearsome looking woman. His plaintive, and really slightly desperate question had been met with a suitably gallic shrug of the shoulders and fairly disinterested 'Quoi?'. This had not gone down well with the Air Commodore who had been inhaling in anticipation of a fearful riposte when Ellen had had the sense to intervene with her best schoolgirl gallic.

'Monsieur would very much like to know a quelle heure le repas est-il?'

'Ah madam, le dejeuner n'est pas avant une heure,' she replied disdainfully.

'Una? Una? Una who?' interjected the Air Commodore, his tummy rumbling audibly. 'Who's she then, the chef?'

'No sir, Una I mean une heure is one o'clock,' explained Ellen, trying to suppress a giggle.

'One o'clock, one o'clock! What sort of time for lunch is that? Wot, wot, wot, wot!' Exploded the Air Commodore, glancing at his multi-faced chronograph which pinged with immaculate, if disappointing, timing to inform him that it was precisely midday. 'Ah, well I suppose the sun's sufficiently over the yard arm, I should think eh what? Who's for a pre-luncheon snorter? G and bally T, I should cocoa.' And before anyone could reply he began to stride towards what he assumed, amongst the motley selection of wooden buildings, was the officer's mess in pursuit of the aforementioned beverage. 'What's for lunch anyway?' he demanded of the orderly as he walked, the reply of which was not audible, but caused him to berate the orderly further 'Les Cargo, Les Cargo? Is *he* the bally chef then, or the entertainment? Wot, wot,' and with that he was gone.

Ellen pulled a face at Fitch, as if to say: see what I have to work with. Fitch just growled to himself.

'Oh well, I guess we should try and find Sir Lushthorpe and make ourselves useful,' and with that and an affirmative meow from Mrs Tickle III tucked contentedly under Fitch's arm, they turned about heel and headed towards the tracks of the mighty Tri Trans-Continental Express.

The walk to the rocket took longer than they expected as the massive edifice was surrounded by many service vehicles, and a veritable shanty town of forges, workshops, steam cranes and assorted construction paraphernalia. When they eventually arrived, they were greeted by a clearly impatient looking Sir Grenville Lushthorpe, all bones, teeth and wild hair and the equally eccentric person of the King's Astronomer Royal – Scarlett Carshalton with mismatched shoes and green lab coat with a purple and blue striped jumper untidily pulled over the top.

'What time do you call this?' demanded Sir Lushthorpe glaring through a set of triple-lensed optics in a manner even more manic than was usually his way.

'Pre-lunch drinkies time,' giggled Ellen, trying to control herself, 'at least the Air Commodore seems to think so.'

'Lunch is for parrots!' exclaimed Carshalton waving her gloved hands, which gave every appearance of having a miniature telescope attached to every finger.

'No time for any of that! Get on board, we have many, many preparations to make,' muttered Lushthorpe and, as he turned back into the train carriage, a great cloud of steam flooded over them from some unseen pipe overhead. Coughing and trying to see where they were going Fitch, Ellen and Mrs. Tickle III clambered up into the converted saloon car and made after the batty duo, who had headed off along the train towards the complicated scaffolding that supported the enormous rocket.

'Of all the crazy nonsense I've been involved in,' growled Fitch to himself, as he stomped along, but if he thought Lushthorpe hadn't heard he was much mistaken.

'Crazy you say!' rounded the inventor turning on the entry ladder to confront the grizzled soldier. 'Not a bit of it. All makes perfect sense.' He continued up into the body of the metal cylinder as the others hurried to follow. 'Three stage rocket, first stage is the train, eh? Gets us up to speed for take-off, then a ballistic rocket stage and finally a catapult to launch the capsule on to the moon eh, eh? What's crazy about that?' Ellen could barely hold back another giggle but somehow, she did.

'It's just like a caterpillar, when it turns into a rose,' added Carshalton without actually making things any clearer. As Ellen continued to stifle a snigger, she attempted to take in her surroundings now they were inside the rocket proper. It was a kind of steel-clad anteroom, with many pipes, dials and levers all around, and in one corner a rack of cobbled-together looking spacesuits. It also, rather alarmingly considering that launch was due within the day, seemed to still be in the process of being constructed. A whole platoon of engineers, some Albioners, but most clearly local Gauls were welding and hammering and non-specifically engineering in all directions.

'Er, is it actually finished?' enquired Fitch, not looking too impressed.

'Finished!' interjected Carshalton, glancing at him through two of her finger scopes, 'finished is all in the mind of the cheesemonger.'

'Well, it's coming on,' muttered Lushthorpe, trying to ignore the nutty astronomer. 'Probably worth getting an update from madam superviseur though, now you've mentioned it, where is she? Madam Mélasse! Madam Mélasse!'

The shout was taken up amongst the ensemble and after a short while, madam le superviseur Mélasse appeared from behind a stack of oil cans, wrench in hand and grease smeared all over her face.

'Oui monsieur?' she enquired.

'No, I'm fine thank you, I went before boarding,' replied Lushthorpe confusingly, 'How's the rocket progressing? Tell me you have at least finished the second stage release mechanism; we are in very big trouble if that's not working.'

The gauloise was about to reply, when a deep and ominous horn sounded, rattling anything that wasn't firmly screwed down which, as usual, was almost everything.

'Good grief,' exclaimed Ellen, 'what on earth is that?'

'Ah, zat,' began Madam Mélasse as all around her engineers began to down tools and shuffle towards the exit. 'Zat is ze lunchtime 'orn, it is time for ze break.'

'Break!' exploded Lushthorpe, 'we've no time for a break'

'It is ze union rules, monsieur. You understand of course, it's is time for ze brie and ze burgundy.'

'We really don't have time for any of that,' exclaimed Lushthorpe, 'we must launch today, soon, understand, verstehen, komprenu?'

'Aujourd'hui?' replied the supervisor looking extremely sceptical, 'she will not launch today I am very much afraid.'

Seeing the look of mild concern on Ellen, Fitch, Carshalton and even Mrs Tickle's faces at this statement, Lushthorpe felt inclined to defend his, if not greatest, then certainly biggest, invention to date.

'Afraid, afraid, no, non, nein! We must allay your fears!' he chuntered loudly in a not particularly convincing way and to help emphasis his point he picked up a complicated looking spanner and began to wave it around. 'Allay, allay I tell you!'

'Allez?' enquired madam la superviseur suddenly looking very excited.

'Yes, ja, jes, si – allay, allay! Nothing to worry about, allay!' confirmed Lushthorpe, his tool waving becoming ever more frantic.

'Very well monsieur,' with this she turned after the disappearing engineers and clapped her hands in a commanding fashion.

'Allez, allez! Vite, vite, nous allons, nous allons!'

'Yes, yes,' encouraged Lushthorpe feeling a bit more relieved that people seemed to be listening to him finally. 'Gosh very keen, yes, vite vite allay all those naughty gaulish fears.'

It was at this point that Ellen, given her slightly better command of Gaulish, began to look rather alarmed as all the engineers left and madam superviseur closed and gave every appearance of having locked the exit hatch behind her.

'Erm, I'm not sure that means, what you think it means,' she began, but Lushthorpe dismissed her with a wave of his spanner and busied himself with a control panel. Seeing that he wasn't about to listen she turned to the lady astronomer, but she was also fussing around with a kind of reciprocating lunar sextant affair, or similar, and also waved her away.

'Oh dear,' muttered Ellen, turning to Fitch, but he could only offer a shrug.

It was at this point that, with a great lurch, the trains began to move.

'I say,' exclaimed Lushthorpe looking up with the most fearful expression from his control panel, 'what's going on? Why on earth is the train moving?!'

'Well I was trying to tell you – allay in Gaulish means, well, go,' muttered Ellen, moving to the hatch and looking around frantically for some way to open it. 'Oh no,' she added.

'What now!' wailed Lushthorpe.

'Er, is there any way to open the hatch from within, it seems rather lacking in any form of, erm, handle,' she gave it another look over just to make sure, but her total tally of portal opening type lever thingies was adding up to exactly none.

'Well now, one doesn't want to be opening that by mistake during the flight now does one?' chided Lushthorpe, although it was dawning on him that it might not have been such a bad idea to include a door handle after all. Before he could add anything else, a mighty roar and a violent rattle shook the rocket and it became obvious to one and all that they were picking up speed at an alarming rate.

'Was that the...' started Fitch, but Lushthorpe cut him off.

'The rocket motor firing up, yes, I rather think it was.'

'So that means...' started Fitch again, but once more he was curtailed.

'We are launching whether we like it or not,' stated Lushthorpe glancing urgently around the room in all directions.

'What are you looking for exactly?' asked Ellen, keen to help as always.

'Er the Air Commodore, is Loveboat not amongst our number? I could have sworn I saw him.'

'No, he's bloody having lunch!' growled Fitch.

'Him too? Well who's going to fly the bally thing then?' wailed Lushthorpe, as everyone looked at everyone else with desperation. Finally, all eyes alighted on Ellen.

'Who me?' she gulped, 'Well I'm game to give it a try, if you like,' offered Ellen, 'how hard can it be?' All stared at her wide-eyed, but before anyone could add anything further Mrs Tickle suddenly leapt from Fitch's arms and headed towards the rack of spacesuits. The whole rocket shook again, and it was clear that there was no going back now.

'Spacesuits, everyone now!' commanded Fitch, following the space cat's lead, and no one seemed inclined to contradict him.

Barely had the motley crew hauled on mis-fitting and ramshackle spacesuits when there came a number of loud popping sounds from outside the rocket.

'What now?' cried Carshalton, who had found it impossible to get her telescope-festooned hands into the suit and had, very reluctantly, been forced to remove them.

'Connection bolts released,' explained Lushthorpe, 'we are no longer attached to the train, we must get to the bridge and fire the lift boosters, or all will be lost.' Quite what was to be gained by this, considering there were only the five of them aboard, no one had the heart to ask, but clamber up ladders and through hatches they all went, until they arrived, sweaty and out of breath on the bridge. This was a huge steel and glass bullet head at the very pinnacle of the rocket. To the front they could see the great eastern Gaulish plains stretching out before them, inscribed by the three parallel tracks of the TTCE and, somewhat more alarmingly, a range of snow-peaked mountains advancing towards them rapidly. Smoke and steam were pouring up from the three steam locomotives and it was clear they were hurtling forward at incredible speed, the like of which none of them had ever experienced before.

'Looks like madam supervisor is really allezing it now!' muttered Ellen hauling herself into the pilot's seat and strapping herself in. Lushthorpe, Carshalton and Fitch did likewise in seats arranged behind her in the cabin.

'No time to lose, are we all secured?' yelled Lushthorpe over the increasing din, and when all the cries where in the affirmative he hit a large red button next to his chair with a gloved hand. Nothing additional seemed to happen at this point, so Lushthorpe hit it again. Still nothing. Finally, Lushthorpe battered it like a mad toddler with the spanner he had brought from the cabin and this time something did happen.

With an incredible roar the main engine of the rocket screamed into life and the most incredible g-forces slammed them into their seats as the whole contraption began to lift away from the train. Ellen pulled frantically and grimly at the controls and, despite the great shaking and whining of metal from all around, the rocket appeared to be actually ascending as intended. The acceleration was relentless, making it hard for any of them to move or even talk, although for some reason known only to herself, Carshalton offered a cryptic: 'That's hit the nail on the bullet' through rattling teeth.

As they continued to rush skywards the light outside the cabin began to change, the blue of the afternoon sky being replaced with ever darkening tones.

'How are we doing?' yelled back Ellen as she continued to grip the controls like grim death.

'Fairly splendid, thank you,' came the juddering reply from Lushthorpe as an urgent pinging noise began to emanate from an instrument panel near the astronomer Carshalton.

'What the dickerty-moose does that mean?' she enquired peering at the panel through yet another telescope she had acquired from somewhere.

'Ah that means we need to release the rocket stage,' pronounced Lushthorpe, who began to look all around him with increasing levels of desperation.

'Lost something?' growled Fitch.

'Er, well, there should be a second stage release button here, er somewhere...' his voice tailed of as the pinging continued to, well, ping, ever more urgently. '...er, perhaps they haven't installed that yet.'

'Oh for heaven's sake,' muttered Fitch, 'is there another way to release the rocket stage?'

'Well there is probably a manual release, somewhere, big red lever, hard to miss...' Before Lushthorpe could even finish his sentence, Fitch had undone his restraints and was, with a huge sigh, working with the g-forces to head back out of the cabin.

'Big red lever you say,' he growled as he departed.

'Well probably, you know, if they got around to...' but Fitch didn't hear him as he moved jerkily from hand hold to hand hold, hauling himself back towards the rear of the rocket. The jolting, rattling clamour from all around him was almost over-powering. But somehow, he put one step for a man, one giant step for some other folk after another and hauled himself back along the body of the monster looking for a big red lever. Finally, just as he thought he could bear it no longer he saw one, suitably red, suitably big, set in a brass panel at the very back of the final room.

'This better be it,' he wheezed as with all his might he fought the g-forces to fall as close as he could to the lever, and pull it, only for it to come clean off the wall in his hand.

'Oh bugger,' he muttered, but there seemed little choice but to discard the lever and work his way slowly and with incredible difficulty back to the cabin.

'Well?' enquired Lushthorpe as he finally got his head back through the cabin door.

'Slight problem,' he growled, 'seems someone forgot to install the lever, came off in me hand.'

'Oh,' muttered Lushthorpe, sounding extremely deflated.

'I don't want to interrupt,' started Ellen, trying to sound as polite as she could, 'but I'm struggling a wee bit, and there are some rather large mountains coming up. Is there any way we can, er you know, get off?'

'Well, I'm not really sure,' began Lushthorpe sounding rather resigned to crashing at this point.

'What about the catapult?' interjected Carshalton, 'wouldn't that fire us to flipperdy and deploy the chuteyparawhatsit?'

'Catapult?' growled Fitch sounding unconvinced, 'is there a button for that?' Lushthorpe looked all around, but was forced to concede that he certainly couldn't see one.

'Er... um... er...' he began, but Fitch was having none of it.

'Where's this effing catapult?' he shouted over the din. By this point it was all Lushthorpe could do to point forlornly at a trapdoor in the floor. 'Right, here we go.' Muttered Fitch, and he hauled the cover off and leaned himself over to look into the hole thus opened.

'I can see the elastic, but how do I release it?' shouted Fitch over the din of the rocket.

'Pull the ratchet down,' yelled Lushthorpe by return, without really thinking through the consequences. And so, Fitch reached with all his might and pulled the pin, which immediately fired the catapult throwing him like a raggedy doll against the cold, hard, unyielding cabin wall. He was unconscious before he could even curse the engineer that had failed to install both the second stage release lever, and the catapult firing button, before buggering off for brie and burgundy. And believe me dear reader, he had a really good curse in mind.

It was a while later that, having somehow, against all the odds survived the premature ejection of the cabin and the, better late than not at all, deployment of the retardation parachutes, which halted their fall, whilst still knocking them all unconscious, that Ellen Hall came to, hauled herself out of her seat and began to look for the others. As smoke and the distant crackle of fire filled the cabin, she shook a delirious Lushthorpe into consciousness and with Carshalton's help began to drag him from the twisted metal of the rocket into the rocky landscape outside.

Fitch was harder to find, but eventually, with help from Mrs Tickle's keener nose, they found him buried in angular shards of metal. His suit pierced in multiple locations and his right arm hanging limply in his suit. All hands and paws were required to pull his unconscious frame clear and lay him gingerly into a hastily constructed bed, made of torn parachute silk. With care they removed his suit, to prevent him overheating and, as they hauled it off, Ellen was surprised to find that behind one of the bigger gashes in the suit was a, now pierced and creased, children's picture book. She pulled it out carefully, since it seemed that Fitch obviously treasured it greatly.

Lushthorpe, who had been in quite a daze and muttering about dreams and déjà vu, slumped down beside her as she began to thumb idly through the book.

'This book may have saved his life,' she mumbled to herself tracing the hole where the metal had been embedded, aware that she could possibly hear an ornithopter or other aircraft in the distance, a rescue party perhaps. 'Look how it was nearly pierced through,' she showed the page to Sir Grenville, who seemed deep in thought and not keen to indulge in her book club discussion just yet. However, Ellen's eyes began to widen as she realised that she was staring at something very familiar. Labelled, extremely cryptically "EAR-MOO B" the double-page drawing featured a circle of gantries, towers and other constructions around a large circular floor of exotic looking material. The setting was the desert somewhere and she gave a little gasp, as she realised where she'd seen this edifice before.

'Oh, we'll never get to the moon now!' moaned Sir Lushthorpe with near complete despondency, gazing forlornly at the twisted scrap metal of the once magnificent rocket. So grief-stricken was he that he didn't notice either the first of the rescue party hurrying towards them, nor Ellen's whispered reply, gazing at the pages of Fitch's book.

'Actually, I think I might know a way, but first we might need to find some pirates in the desert.'

To be continued

XVI

Welcome to Aeropa

Oh, where do all the airships go?
When the moorings slip
And the storm wind blows.
When their tethers break
And they crack their 'foils?
Oh, where do all the airships go?
Folke Song of Olde Albion - Anon

Rusty Inglemop was not having a good week. It had started well enough as she and her bestest Chimpanzee pal Belistranka had arranged a relaxing airship trip over the Lanchester estuary. Unfortunately, the problems had started when, determined to be early, she departed before an electro-gram had arrived which would have informed her that the joy ride was to be put on hiatus due to inclement weather. The hammering rain, dense fog and gale-a-blowin' might have been a clue, but Rusty and simian companion had pressed on undaunted, making it over the gangway into the unmanned pleasure dirigible just as a particularly savage gust snapped its inadequate moorings and blew them all away.

This had been four days ago, and since then she and Bella had seen nothing but the inside of the, unfuelled and uncontrollable, airship and the dense grey storm clouds outside. They thanked their lucky stars that the ship had been stocked with emergency rations and drinking water. They fashioned beds from blankets and played cards, when they weren't scared out of their wits, and prayed to all the gods and none that they would arrive somewhere safely, eventually. And eventually they did, although they didn't know it, as they were fast asleep at the time on the benches of the small cabin, the wind having finally eased and the airship having cozied up to something not too hard, and not too soft.

Rusty was startled awake by an old woman with unkempt hair, a loose blue tabard with a gold chain around her waist, a medallion around her neck and a blue and white tea towel tied to her head, shaking her furiously.

'Wake up, wake up, you must wake up,' muttered the woman in an overly loud stage whisper.

'Walaharrrgh?' squawked Rusty undiplomatically, as she recoiled from the woman, who gave the appearance of some sort of vagabond nun, malnourished and unkempt. When she saw Rusty and the ape awakening crone also backed off, clearly uncertain how they might react to her presence. This allowed Rusty to gather her thoughts somewhat, so she added a more useful 'Where are we?'

'Aeropa,' hissed the woman through yellow teeth and then added more stealthily 'do you have a clan yet?' She looked around anxiously as voices could be heard in the distance. Now Rusty was well read but had never come across anywhere called Aeropa.

'Where is...?' she started to form another question, but the hag cut her off.

'You are not safe here without weapons or a clan defend you.' There were footsteps on a gangway not so far away now, and Rusty felt a flutter of panic. 'If you have food or fuel, then pledge it to me and the Church of Emitters can protect you.'

'There is n-n-no fuel,' stammered Rusty, finding her mouth very dry and palms sweaty, 'we ate all the food, b-b-but I have a few b-b-barley sugars,' she reached into her pocket and brought out three wax paper wrapped sweets, only one of which had been previously sucked.

'Will you give them to me willingly?' hissed the woman, her eyes bulging ever wider.

'Of course, here they are,' she handed them over and the woman grabbed them greedily, but then her eyes turned kinder.

'Then welcome to the Church of the Emitters of Rabbi F Fatz,' and as the footsteps grew alarmingly loud, she quickly hauled the square medallion from around her neck and looped it over Rusty's head. 'Now hide the monkey!'

Rusty was about to explain how Belistranka was actually an ape when without ceremony the woman threw a blanket over said primate and almost simultaneously the door to the gondola flew open to reveal another strange and irksome character peering in through the shadows.

'Does this ship have a clan?' he drawled in the most monotonous voice Rusty had ever had the misfortune to hear and it had to be said that the body attached to it was equally unfortunate. His eyes were sunk and reddened, his body hunched grotesquely so he was almost on all fours, his tattered clothing all grey and gathered around him in a dishevelled manner. The man, if it was such, was clearly emaciated and what little greasy hair he had, he tugged at constantly with a bony hand.

'Go away Sneer,' commanded the women, seemingly not fearing the hideous apparition. 'She's with the Emitters now, all her food and fuel are freely pledged.' He glared at them, taking in the medallion around Rusty's neck that she held towards him now as if it was talisman to ward off the evil eye. He seemed clearly disappointed at this and continued to knot his hair in a quite disgusting way.

'Sneer is not my name,' he drawled, 'But you shall not know it, you nor your Martian friends. They slice you up you know,' and with that cryptic, and slightly morbid, pronouncement he turned his head and slunk out of the doorway.

Rusty felt a shiver of disgust wriggle its way down her spine. 'Urgh, what was that? He looked like a rat or something.'

'Rat is the right word,' said the woman, noisily extracting one of the barley sugars and which she then popped in her mouth and proceeded to suck nosily. Through the sucks she held out a dirty and skinny hand, 'I'm Fatima by the way, Fatima Fatz.'

'Oh, like the rabbi you mentioned, are you related?' The woman laughed in a slightly manic way and shook her head vigorously.

'Of course not, silly, my real name is Susan, that's just my Emitter name.'

By this point, sensing the coast to be clear, Belistranka tentatively emerged from under the blanket and nervously sniffed the air. Fatima or Susan, or whatever her name was held out a hand to her too.

'Greetings, you are also welcome monk...' Rusty cut her short.

'She's not a monkey, she's a chimpanzee, an ape, just like you.' But Belistranka was used to being mis-speciesed and shook the offered hand anyway. Rusty squinted at the square medallion, it was a fairly crude piece of tin with letters stamped on it in an amateurish way. It read "EMIT TRAP" in large letters and below that "F FATZ RAB.", although the lettering was weird, like some kind of foreign language. The e for example looked more like a 3 and the p like a q. Susan/Fatima's eyes glistened as she saw her reading the words, and a smile creased her wrinkled face.

'It was a sign from our lord and saviour,' she eulogised in the reverent tones of an elderly Sunday School teacher. 'Emit trap, send out from the trap. The trap being this place that imprisons us all,' she explained raising her flabby arms to indicate their current location, 'F Fatz Rab, now some people think that Rab might be a name, but I, like most, choose to believe it's short for rabbi, which means teacher.' She sat herself down on one of the benches, clearly settling in for a long yarn, so Rusty and Bella did likewise. Thus beseated, the crone proceeded to explain how the founder of the church had come across this message amongst the ashes of a fire on the floor of an airship. Taking it as a sure sign that F Fatz would surely come one day and rescue them all. The ashes soon blew away, but the message was seared in her mind and now in medallions Emitters all wore.

'Where exactly is *this* place, this trap as you call it?' interrupted Rusty, wanting to clear this point up early doors.

'Ah, my manners,' she glanced out the window, 'I see the cloud is lifting a little, I should show you around,' And with that she sprang up and moved to the doorway, beckoning them to follow. Cautiously she glanced out to make sure the rat man had gone and then hobbled outside.

Rusty and Bella shrugged at each other and then followed her out of the door to where a loose gangplank had been laid up to their gondola and a rope attached connecting them to another airship, and then another and another and another beyond that. In every direction they saw balloon after balloon, every type of dirigible, blimp, gasbag, skyhook, Montgolfier and rockoon; their gondolas, baskets and cars floating freely or lashed crudely into larger structures, a veritable floating city of jetsam. Fati-Suse noted their slack-jawed gaze and opened her arms proudly, if resignedly, and declared,

'Welcome to where all the lost airships go, welcome to Aeropa!'

Feeling both elated and off-the-scale terrified, Rusty was preparing to ask a thousand questions when her spinning train of thought was interrupted by a dark and ominous horn blowing. This in turn caused all the questions to get muddled up in her mouth and all she was able to say was, 'Wherned ger whatty issy dat?'

Belistranka widened her eyes and gave her a sideways glance of disapproval, but old Fati-Suse seemed to comprehend the garbled query.

'Ah the horn of discovery,' she declared 'another stray has arrived, a bit more valuable than yours I wager, and this time with no souls aboard, so there must be a chuntering amongst the clans.' Before Rusty could ask any follow up questions she turned and clapped her hands excitedly, 'shall we go and see?' The others raised no objection, mostly due to being completely confused, which she took as pretty much full consent. 'Oh goody. We'll need a disguise for your monk... oh I mean ape though. Animals tend to get eaten around here, lots of rather hungry people.' And with that and a 'wait here' she scurried away.

'Her name is Belistranka!' yelled Rusty after her, but to no obvious effect. She turned to the slightly annoyed looking ape and offered her most consolatory face. 'Sorry old girl, I think I've got us into a bit of a pickle. Ah though, hopefully not with actual pickle, err no, sorry, not funny, oh dear,' Rusty thought it best be quiet at this point lest she stick her foot any further into her cakehole. Bella just rolled her eyes and shrugged her hairy shoulders at this, but then seemed to have a brainwave and tugged Rusty back into the cabin, her eyes filled with purpose.

When Susi-Fatz finally returned, it seemed that her idea of a disguise was simply a pair of the grubby blue tabards, gold waist chains and medallions that she herself was wearing. Oh, and a pair of white and blue tea towels similar to her own, one of which she tied over the ape's head with a length of cord. Having dressed both Belistranka and Rusty thus, she stood back to admire her handiwork, popped another barley sugar in her mouth and slurped 'Shall we go see the new arrival?' before turning heel and shuffling off towards where the horn had intoned its baleful wail only minutes earlier. Seeing that they had not much of a choice our two castaways simply followed gingerly behind, along the gangplanks lashed between the many stricken vessels. Despite her age Susi-Fatty moved with the ease of much familiarity between the vessels and had to pause many times to enable the others to catch up, as they were not so sure footed amongst the swaying and jolting ships. However, this short journey finally allowed Rusty to ungarble her questions and one by one she started to get some answers, however what she heard filled her with increasing amounts of cold dread.

It seemed that they were indeed in the city of lost airships, floating high in the air, over a giant volcano surrounded by countless acres of frigid ocean. The volcano they cheerily called Odark the Oppressor, and its hot upstream was what held them all in this odd place with very little chance of escape. Below was Hobson's choice of molten lava or crashing ocean and all winds, currents and airstreams seemed to suck with a grinding inevitability to this singularity. Any airship without power caught in the wind from any place on the globe would end up here sooner or later. It could take days, or decades, but the result was the same and those who survived this ordeal now had little choice but to forage and grub an existence amongst this maze of balloons. Their bodies weakening as their minds collapsed with the inescapable futility of it all. Reading between the tether ropes it seemed most people unfortunate enough to be incarcerated here were either slowly wasting away or losing their minds or a combination of the two. This feeling was reinforced when a muttering and frantic woman barged past them dragging a crazy-knotwork of rope behind her. In truth the entirety of the variegated tied cables was so long it took nearly a full minute to finally snake past them, and Rusty and Bella had been forced into a veritable tap dance to avoid treading on it. Susany-F answered their question even before they had asked it,

'Probably a dangler,' she pronounced sagely as if it was the most ordinary thing, 'they lower themselves down hoping to reach the ground.' She turned and began to lead them onwards again, 'It's too far though,' she called back over her shoulder, 'and they'd only burn anyway, or drown, or the middle one.'

On this cheery note they moved on, and gradually began to pass more people forcing Bella to tug her tea towel down further over her head in an effort to look vaguely human. Mind you that wasn't particularly difficult amongst this bunch of weirdoes. In fact, no one gave her more than a passing glance. It was truly a wonder how anybody survived up here, thought Rusty, but somehow survive they did. Laying traps to snare birds, catching rainwater, growing seeds caught on the breeze and rearing and eating any livestock careless enough to be caught on an airship lost to the elements. And, of course, dividing up the spoils of any bountiful dirigibles that arrived on the scolding wind. The rules of this seemed to be that if you arrived with a ship, it was yours to keep or barter away for the protection of a clan, but if the ship was unmanned then different rules applied depending on the exact locality with which it collided. It seemed this latest arrival had fallen in a kind of no-folk's land, so the Grublins, the Brotherhood of the Albatross, The Fallers, The Ascenders and the Emit Trappers (plus a few diehard loners) all had to argue the toss amongst themselves in something called a Chuntering. The rules of which seemed so arcane and convoluted that Rusty gave up listening to the explanation almost immediately. In any case she could observe it now with her own eyes and hear with her own ears as there they all were assembled before her, haggling loudly in their skewbald mix of clan colours and varied tongues. In amongst this rainbow midden, Rusty thought she glimpsed the monochrome rags of Sneer leering at them with his bloodshot gaze, but before she could be sure he vanished into the throng. Oh, how much she wanted to be gone from this place and return to the cheery, if smelly, comfort of the chimpanzee orphanage. Then, as Fatima-S pointed out the new airship arrival which had given rise to this cacophony, it dawned on her gawking ganglions that it might actually be a road to their escape.

The ship that the throng of air dwellers were getting so worked up about was a beast of a balloon. Fully 800 feet long and what you might call a classic zeppelin in shape, on the face of it a fairly utilitarian military dirigible, if a little damaged, perhaps from a battle. Rusty though had studied airship design and knew more about what this one usually had aboard. She reached out and grabbed Suzy-Fat's arm.

'How much do you want to leave this place?' she whispered, fearful that the animated mob of crazies might overhear.

'I *will* leave, when F Fatz Rab comes to emit us from this trap,' answered Fat Susan in rote fashion, clearly indoctrinated by years of delusion.

'Yes, yes, but what if we could leave sooner? I know something about that airship,' she hissed. 'We studied them in technical college.' She pulled F-Susan closer before she could respond and added, 'It's an aircraft carrier.'

'So, what are you saying? There may be planes aboard? With engines?' Susan gazed at the battered zeppelin with fresh insight, Rusty thought she saw the welling of a small tear as she nodded her affirmation. 'Ah but even if it were true, who can fly it? Can you? I can't. I really, really can't'

'No,' conceded Rusty, 'but...' Before she could elaborate she was cut off as Belistranka, clearly getting more than a little frustrated with pretending to be something as daft as a human, threw off her tea towel head garb and pulled out the flare pistol she had rescued from their airship and started waving it around threateningly.

'...but she can,' concluded Rusty, indicating the tooled-up ape. Realising that she had no real option but to go along with Bella's play, she started yelling 'The ape's got lose!' whilst flailing her arms around, 'and she's got a gun!' She turned to Bella and whispered sotto voce, 'Is it actually loaded?' the ape just shrugged and continued to wave it, baring her teeth and any lunatic who dared to stand in their way. Rusty and a slightly reluctant, but hopeful Sussy-Fats followed on behind then, her face the picture of complete incomprehension.

'Can your monk... ah, I mean ape fly a plane?' enquired FaSu looking decidedly dubious.

'Yep, certainly can,' replied Rusty, 'She was trained in Rusland to pilot kamikaze rockets,' And then added swiftly, as Susan the Fat gazed at her even more wide-eyed than usual, 'don't ask!'

And so somehow the nutty nun, the ex-draughtswoman with a poor sense of danger and the flare gun toting suicide bomb pilot chimpanzee, made their way onto the YAS Akron despite howls of impotent rage from the Aeropean cohort. Then with the calm efficiency you would expect of a Russkie trained chimp pilot, Belistranka located, lowered and started one of the seemingly entirely airworthy triplanes and, with incredible skill, flew it free from its complicated trapeze and skyhook apparatus, leaving the bizarre floating shanty town of Aeropa behind them. As they banked away, by chance, Rusty caught a glimpse of herself and her Emitter Church medallion in the reflection of the plane canopy and gave a little gasp of realisation. The nagging feelings that she'd had in the back of her mind since meeting Fatima (who used to be Susan) were confirmed. The miracle of the burning paper was not particularly divine in its origination. Emit Trap Ffats Rab when you viewed it in the mirror was as mundane as you could possibly imagine, saying simply "Part Time Bar Staff" presumably to be followed by the word "Required" as part of an advertisement on a pleasure cruiser that had caught fire and was subsequently lost to the winds of destiny. She thought better of mentioning this to the dewy-eyed Susan though as, under Bella's skilful control, they broke free of the cloud cover and saw the glinting peaks of the ocean below them. Which ocean it was and where they might be heading, they knew not. But the salty air of freedom smelt good, they had a plane that could fly against the wind and thus expedite their escape them from all the madness that lay behind them. Or so they thought.

In the ape flare gun waving frenzy to get aboard, they had failed to notice the pointy-faced, snivelling, grey shape of the rat man slip in behind them and attach himself like a limpet - a tedious, grey, rat-faced limpet - to their plane's under-carriage. Where he now hung below them cackling his monotonous cackle and dribbling like the twisted mad rodent-a-like-thing he was. Wherever they were headed, it seemed Snook, for that was his real name, was coming along for the ride.

To be continued.

XVII

The Battle of Turnip Field

[This article, written by P.G. Basilthorpe-Stilton OAE, first appeared in the *New Albion Gazette* on 21st June 1839, and was then subsequently revised as a chapter of his memoirs – *The Whole of History and How I Wrote It.* Basilthorpe-Stilton was chief war correspondent for the Gazette (1830 to 1841) and, by all accounts, a right pompous ass.]

When history shines its gaudy limelight of posterity on the humble actions and, indeed, actors of the Great Martian War, there will be few scenes less unilluminating than the incredible action of noble Albioners that I witnessed upon Turnip Field. Every incident relating to that remarkable battle is a reflection of our great and noble character, even the bits that didn't go so well. In fact, perhaps those bits the most. Nevertheless, it was a great and resonating victory that brought about the downfall of the demons. It has been said that before Turnip Field we knew no victories, and after it we pretty much kicked their butt all the way back to Mars. Before this day we were lame sparrows lead by blind donkeys, but after the great event it was the other way around or, dare I say it, vice versa.

How was this great victory achieved and who were the stout-of-heart Albioners who brought it home to us? Well let me try and set it out for you, in a way that even you might just about be able to comprehend.

And lo the curtain swings aside on the morning of 18th June in the year of our lord 1839 revealing a cool grey mist. Enter stage right, (although in truth it could have been stage left, I was still somewhat waylaid by a splendid breakfast repast at the nearby Hotel Phlegmonger) General Ferrous-Nut, a soldier of the oldest school. Who would certainly have been a fine figure of a modern warrior if it had not been for his missing eye, his three mechanical limbs, and his iron lung. The bellows for which was transported behind him on a wooden and brass cart towed by a brace of fine asses. Inconvenient for dinner parties most certainly, but otherwise functional enough. Indeed, these days he is considered more mechanism than man, but nevertheless his strategy deducing grey matter is still as bright as ever it was, gleaming out mischievously through his one good eye. He is the great chess master, laying out his chess board, arranging his chess pieces, for this metaphorical game of badminton. Performing alongside him in the chilly, camouflage-bedecked command tower, dextrously avoiding his cantankerous mechanical appendages – was the winsome and sharp-beaked Mrs Hildenbrand-Fogg, war cabinet undersecretary, or was it under cabinet war secretary? Bah! History cares not for such frippery! In her strong arms the purring feline ball of fluff that comes by the name of Mrs Tickle, the first of the Holomatron-detecting cats. There not just to look decorative, but to secure the safety of the humans by sniffing out the alien hard light machines, that might otherwise walk undetected and, indeed, unsmelt amongst them. The final player in my troika of triumph is the learned Professor Archibald Lushthorpe, inventor royale and overseer of *the grand design*. Together, surrounded by a coterie of lieutenants, sub-lieutenants, junior under sub-lieutenants and various ancillaries, orderlies and lackeys, then have plotted and schemed. Crafting their Martian fly trap over many days of hard toil. And now as the mist slowly evaporates off the rolling Albionshire fields, it is time for the spring to be sprung.

Let me now lay out the stage whereupon our fine actors are preparing their craft, with a finery of detail that will make you feel you are yourself present this balmy summer morning. Now as a hunter knows, every good trap needs the perfect lure, and on this particular day the "Lure" was the Queen's own retinue! Now let me reassure you this was not the real contingent of airships, caravans and miscellaneous pomp, but instead a vast painted canvas, befitting our humble theatre trope. It was hung at the far end of the field on rangy scaffolding, in the earnest hope of attracting our fiendish foe onto the battlefield, imagining all the while they had the Queen cornered ready to be devoured in their salivating chops. Little were they to know that this was merely a ruse to pull them onto the playing field which had been rigged, in no uncertain terms, to favour the home team. The many surprises in store for them I will not spoil, but rather allow each to blossom in turn as the noble tale continues to be told.

Now the great stage manager in the sky pulls his taut ropes and summons the disk of the mid-summer sun into the azure blue waters above, and its long morning shadows play across our course brown acre. The birds of the fields skip from hedgerow to hedgerow unaware of the coming drama, a russet brown fox sniffs the air. Does she know something of the coming storm? Perhaps, as in an eyeblink she is seen no more, and we can determine our first glimpse of the dreaded adversary. It is a trusted sub-under-junior lieutenant o' the watch that espies them first and his cry sends up a holler, "Enemy ho!", and all eyes strain for confirmation. Sure enough, there it is, the ominous great ellipse of a Martian war wheel, belching acrid black soot with abandon as it cares not for who sees it. Rolling ever on, crushing all beneath its iron rim, fully two hundred feet in height, it towers above any circular construct of homo sapiens. Besides this cannon beriddled colossus the next to be observed are ten or more heat ray toting tripods, their ovoid heads of gleaming exotic metal reflecting, in horrid splendour, the mortal sun as evil insects. And the last to emerge onto our ruddy brown patch are the terrible foot soldiers of the red planet. The small tottering army of Martian warriors in gilded spacesuits, beholden much as a legion of ants at the feet of their awesome mechanisms. So it is that our players are all present and the play itself is ready to move from mere prologue and enter its first great act. An act we shall call, for clarity's sake, Act One! The General is nervous, his mechanical arms seem to squabble amongst themselves to extract his pocket watch and allow a measure of the exactitude of this noble time to be taken. Professor Lushthorpe shuffles impatiently, but he is soon to be allowed respite, the General finally manages to see the correct hour and he turns to his trusted number two.

"It is time. Unleash the flying monkeys of war!" To witness the speaking of such a noble address causes my heart to skip a beat, a bleary tear of endeavour moistens my eye as the signal flags of destiny are hoisted. Even Mrs H-F and the feline Tickle are on tenterhooks as we all shield our eyes whilst looking to the east for a first glimpse of our dawn crusaders. For a moment there is palpable angst. The Martian's fearsome engines are so near now their ominous progress shakes our tower. Have the monkeys swung back into their trees in search of a banana or similar simian treat? No, fear not stout Albioners, for we hear them even before we see them. Exploiting a weakness amongst the hideous would be usurpers, used only to crushing the lesser beings of their colonies underfoot, that has deprived them of weapons with elevation and accuracy to attend to heavier-than-air flying machines, they swoop. Coming directly from the sun for further advantage the first of the four-winged aeroplanes appear. Each vessel piloted by a gang of bonobo monkeys trained over many hours to fly with one true purpose only, or as close to that as they could get. The quadplanes are delicate canvas on wood affairs, flighty moths fleeing the Sun's flame much against their set nature, however their payloads lack delicacy in equal measure.

Suspended beneath each kite is the full trunk of an Albion Oak, hung as if a giant's trapeze, surfeit only the lithe, if large, acrobat. With reasonable organisation they make for the tripods that are their prey, but the game is afoot now, and the enemy are waking to their challenge. Fiery heat rays of sickening orange and purple lace the previously unrent sky. Will the monkeys panic as reality vows to burn their underbellies? Well, yes they will, but even in the chaos they begin to find their mark. The first oak hits a tripod and it teeters and falls, a mighty huzzah is lifted amongst the many tiered ranks of lieutenants, a great unleashing of pent-up fury. A blow for humanity, nay a blow for primates of any description the world over. Nay nay and thrice nay surely a blow for all sentient four-limbed, and single headed, fleshy organisms within the galaxy as we know it! With mine very own eyeballs I see the inhuman appliance hit the turnip festooned sod, and another joins it, and another. But woe the brave moths are afire too and many fly hither and thither with little obvious sensibility or design. Nonetheless the plan seems to have born succulent satsumas of success. As the smoke disperses, we see plain that all the tripods lie felled. Another huzzah, less full-blooded, but still hearty erupts from mouths of military folk.

Wait though. Call woah ye huskies of rejoicing, for still the wicked war wheel continues its relentless turn. Crushing now its own fallen as much as the tares of Albion, it cannot, *it will not* be stopped. Or will it?

Permit me if you will a small departure from our *pièce bien faite*, an *amuse-bouche* to refresh the palette before our main course is devoured. Another time, another field where yours truly bore witness to a similar miracle in space and time and, dare I say it, mud. On this occasion a magic trick, the likes of which have never been seen before or since, or even after that. Another expectant crowd, but this time not hunkered in a bestilted bunker, but jovially seated in a temporary grandstand. The spectacle that day was the japery of Senor Apocalypse (not his real name) a four-bit magician of semi-noble bearing, for whom no stunt was too stunted. At his show an, undeniably tangible, curtain hung, in red velvet, fully a quarter furlong across an otherwise devoid plantation. Anticipation aplenty was raised amongst the throng, as with much ado the Senor swept these curtains dramatically apart to reveal an elephant in solitary splendour with nothing else to be seen in all directions, or indeed anywhere. The curtains are then pulled slowly closed again and the pachyderm obscured from general view. Then with great drama and alarm the curtains are set ablaze! They burn intense and black with flickering red, yellow and white flames (perhaps also orange) snarling for seconds that become a minute or possibly two. But lo, as the flames subside and the smoke clears, a miracle is now revealed. For the field is utterly empty, no elephant, no magician, no stagehands, nothing. The crowd are left speechless, amazed, delighted! Many theories are offered, but none can satisfy, the empty field does not lie, it speaks its own plain indigestible veritas. Magic is real.

After our excited trudge back to waiting carriages I wrote up this extravaganza for the Gazette, noting for posterity the name of the technician who had helped devise the illusion, a certain A. Lushthorpe as yet devoid of titles. The man currently only a casual swing of a mace from my current location - the true maestro of Apocalypse's mystery play. So how was the miracle manifested? I will not reveal the magician's art so crudely but suffice to say the endeavour was not without its bloody, sweaty and teary toil, and a steam-powered digging machine. And so, with a thought to the man as yet unprofessored and soon to be recognised by the crown in no uncertain terms we return to our unfolding drama for the second act.

Horror, alarm, more alarm, further horror! The alien's mighty annulus continues to advance, unfettered by Albion clod cleaving limpetwise to its relentless spindle. As the diadem of dire destiny continues to roll forward it is fast approaching the time for Professor Lushthorpe to reverse his great conjuring trick of yore. Before and aft the colossal machine suddenly arise two great rings of fire. Burning hard and bright they repel all the alien insects from them, their triple eyes blinded and stinging. When at last the mighty flames subside, on the great stage there are two new players. Large by the standards of men yet overborn by the vicious circle of Mars, come forth two armoured landships. Slug like in disposition motivated by iron and rubber tracks and belching smoke from their dark, coal-burning bellies they move with inverse alacrity to block the path of the horrible halo fore and aft. This brace of mighty ferrous wedges achieve their goal, the wreath is chocked and cannot revolve further forwards or back. What now? The roar of monkey-manipulated aero engines is upon us once more. Two of the little quadplanes return, with a almighty twisted-metal hawser between them. These are the aces of Albion, the very zenith of primate pilotage permonkeyfied. One kite, its team of bonobos holding it at a death-defying angle flies directly through the very spokes of the aureole as the other passes above it. Thus, entwined in the cable, the engines of the quadplanes chugging furiously, the wheel is pulled from the perpendicular and, its own weight now its downfall, begins to topple. It is said the bigger you are the harder you land on your arse, and its proof is now in the suet-based dessert. The radius is laid low, in a choke of mud, with a mighty tremble that rattles even the iron lung of the General himself, startling his asses. The coronet of the would-be conquerors is thrown to the floor of the throne room, it will not rise again. And yet there is one more twist in our tale as with a series of pops the very turnips of the field begin to explode. One by one these roots are revealed to be, not sons of the soil, but more perfidious parsnips – iron gas grenades - each exploding with guff of wretched brown emittance. This sickly smoke engulfs the hoplites of the opposition, now all but made wretched by our game and one by one they drop to the floor bereft of consciousness. And so, dearly purchased at the expense of the rich blood shed on the memorable occasion; but in the successful issue of this arduous contest the matter is settled.

The war wheel is a wretched wreath to the fallen and now, amongst the inert unconscious fiends, our own foot soldiers dare emerge, scarlet-coated, armed and treading cautiously. But they need not worry as Professors Lushthorpe's tricks have worked with incandescent wonder, and the great metaphorical curtain now swings down to end our opera.

And so, the audience departs, and the stagehands tidy the remains from the field of clay. The unconscious carcasses of the protagonists are gathered, with more care than is deserved, and ferried by horse and cart back to the site of their arrival. With time of the essence they are transmitted by alien magic barely in our ken back to the moon, there to be slung back on their rockets and sent packing into the dark void, in the rough direction of the angry red planet we call Mars - god of war. There had been hollers amongst the unruly mob that the red men should be put to the sword for their many sins, but for some unknown reason they seem to ebb away as the deeds of the miscreants fade quickly from memory. Indeed, many a man cannot seem to even remember how they came to be here in the first place. It is rumoured that this mass absent-mindedness is a side effect of the Professor's malodorous vapour, but even that cannot be determined.

As a postscript I do, however, mull from time to time (over a nice juicy sirloin perhaps) whether we have laid the seeds of our own future tree of calamity. Can the Martian fiends ever find their way back to Earth to finish their foul work? I shudder at this thought, until another glass of finest cognac becalms me. Who can say? For the time being we have achieved what was intended on that inglorious field of turnips: a restoration of peace to Albion and to the Universe. All is well once more, the play has proffered its payoff, the exits are opened by hands unseen and one can step out into the street and breath the damp air of eternal hope once again. Fill your lungs stout folk of Albion, for we are free once more and ever grateful to the fateful fusiliers of the empire who fought so bravely in the pugilistic performance, mythologised for evermore, as the Battle of Turnip Field.

XVIII

Crash Again (Again)!

It had been a mixed bag of fortune for our three heroes following the crash of Sir Grenville Lushthorpe's great rocket in the Gaulish mountains. Fitch had been the worst affected, since he had lost an arm for his trouble, and lay in a rustic hospital convalescing after more than one operation. The Astronomer Carshalton had, rather surprisingly, volunteered to set forth for civilisation in order to try and bring help, should all else fail. In the meantime, Ellen and Mrs. Tickle III had found lodgings in a nearby Gîte and spent the time pondering how to get back to the pirate's lair in the Nubian desert that, thanks to Tom's children's picture book, they now knew was really EAR-MOO B – an giant installation of alien technology, designed to project humans and hardware alike to a corresponding apparatus on the Moon. In fact, it was through this very book that Ellen was flicking again, with Mrs. Tickle purring contentedly on her lap, at Fitch's bedside whilst they all awaited the return of Professor Lushthorpe. The aforementioned inventor having taken a look at Fitch's armless predicament and muttered, "I can probably do something about that" and promptly disappeared. This had been two days ago, and word had reached them that he was intending to call by today with the promised solution.

'What I don't understand though,' ventured Ellen for lack of other topics of conversation, 'Is why no one remembers how we defeated the Martians the first time around?' Fitch had no particular view on the subject, since he was a mass of stiches, sutras and bandages and had been dosed up to the eyeballs on morphine. Still it was rude not to respond so he grunted his agreement. 'I mean it's all here in this kid's picture book,' she slowly turned the pages announcing the contents one after the other, 'Giant machines to send humans to the moon. Holomatron detecting cats, much like our lovely Tickle,' she rubbed Mrs. Tickle III behind the ears, and she murmured happily in response. 'I mean who knew we had commandos on the Moon?' Since absolutely no one did until a mere thirty-four days ago, the other two just shrugged. 'So, what is the actual thing that defeated their invasion?' She flicked again towards the last page hoping that the book would reveal the answer. 'There's this brown gas it seems,' she ventured, lingering on a page showing canisters disguised as turnips being detonated in a muddy field full of Martian tripods and simian-piloted quadplanes. "But the book just describes it as a "Brown emanation that sends the foe into the Land of Nod" – charming for children's bedtime stories I suppose, but from our point of view a little more chemical analysis might have been beneficial.' She sighed a great sigh of frustration. 'Why doesn't anyone remember?' she posed, but before anyone could offer any further gestures of utter cluelessness, Professor Lushthorpe burst into the room accompanied by what appeared to be a swarthy pair of Gaulish mechanics carrying some sort of metal contraption.

'Eureka!' he yelled, I mean 'Well I mean, good morning, you don't smell or anything dear friends. It's Greek or double-dutch or something which means I've fixed it, or you've seen it, or something. Actually, no it doesn't mean either of those things now, what is it again?'

'Good morning Professor,' interrupted Ellen, giggling to herself. 'How are you today?'

'What, yes, er today, lovely thank you kindly,' ranted the Professor, 'but enough of such trivia, I have returned with a new thing!' And with that he waved his arms to encourage the surly Gaulish types to enter with the mass of metal and pistons, that they placed unceremoniously on the bed, right on Fitch's legs.

'Owwww!' growled Fitch, 'Watcha playin' at?' He was about to hurl the heavy metal machinery off the bed with his one surviving arm, but Lushthorpe quickly stepped in to get them to move the construction.

'Not there, not there, it's delicate don't you know! On the side table.' With much muttering and Gaulish annoyance the two hands complied, and the contraption was relocated to the metal table. Here it could be taken in more clearly and it was indeed an odd item. Roughly two-and-a-bit feet long, jointed in two places and with delicate clockwork mechanisms that were currently motionless. All eyes fell firstly on the machine, but since the function of said inert item could not easily be discerned, said eyes eventually turned back to Lushthorpe who had struck a pose of exclamation, arms held aloft.

'Ecce super brachium eius!' he announced. All eyes continued to stare at him, at the machine, and then back to him, a lack of comprehension obvious if no one thought to voice it. His arms and general demeanour slumped in disappointment. 'No Latin scholars amongst you?'

'What do you think?' muttered Fitch under his breath, between sips of a cup of hot sugary tea, 'I'm a mercenary' he nodded to Ellen, 'she's an orphan turned ace pilot and the other one of us is a cat.' He smiled wanly at Mrs Tickle, who shrugged her shoulders insouciantly.

'Well quite, quite, very well in Anglo-Saxon then,' he turned and raised his arms in benediction again, 'Behold... the arm!' At this declaration Fitch spat his mouthful of tea all over the nearest mechanic who was more than a little put out.

Once the Gaul had been pacified with six Francs and a promise of a new overall. Fitch reluctantly acquiesced to have the new "arm" fitted. This process took well over an hour and during that time, Ellen wandered the grounds of the hospital, whilst Mrs Tickle dove in an out of the shrubbery on important "cat" business, trying to hatch a plan to get them all back to the mysterious EAR-MOO installation in the desert. Finally, the cry went out that it was time for the great wind-up and they both trotted back excitedly to Fitch's room. There they found the grizzled mercenary, stripped to the waist, propped up in his bed, with the new mechanical arm attached via various straps, buckles and wires to his right arm stump. He was looking extremely dubiously at the appendage as though some quack was trying to convince him that their snake oil could heal all his problems.

'So how does it work then?' he snarled.

'Well I'm just about to tell you dear boy,' chattered Lushthorpe with manic excitement, reaching forward with a large screwdriver to make a last-minute adjustment. Fitch batted him away with his left arm.

'Well get on with it then, it's already itching!' he moaned, clearly not too comfortable.

'Righty, right,' garbled Lushthorpe clearly getting a bit flustered. 'So, one winds it here,' he pointed to a large folding winder near the shoulder,

'Okay, that seems simple enough,' chirped Ellen, keen to see it in action.

'And here,' he pointed just below that point.

'Right,' muttered Fitch straining to see.

'And here, and here,' he continued to point with the screwdriver at locations of increasingly smaller winders that were much harder to see. Ellen leaned closer, scratching her head.

'And here, here and here.' At this point Fitch was rolling his eyes back in his head and even Ellen's enthusiasm was being stretched to its limits.

'And here.' Lushthorpe appeared to conclude. Fitch sighed loudly,

'Is that it?'

'Yes, yes,' chided Lushthorpe sounding annoyed. 'Oh wait no.' he added having pulled some rough scribbled notes from the pocket of his lab coat.

'Also here, and here... and here' he looked further turning the notes three different ways and trying two different pairs of reading spectacles. 'And here.'

'Is that *all* the winding required?' asked Fitch with a barely disguised note of sarcasm.

'Why certainly,' responded Lushthorpe sounding put out. 'Mind you,' he added, 'You do also need to pump here and here and spin-up this gyroscope.' Seeing that Fitch was beginning to lose the will to live at this point Ellen moved in to try and ease the tension a little.

'Have you written all of this down Professor?' she chirped in her usual ebullient way.

'Well most of it,' confessed the Professor, 'I had to improvise a bit, so some things are still a work in progress.' He tried to advance a second time with the screwdriver, but Fitch pushed him away yet again. 'Erm, well I'll improve it all once we are back in Albion. Anyway, I'd better get winding.' And with that he handed the screwdriver to Ellen, and this time Fitch let him approach and the tedious business of winding, pumping and, indeed, spinning-up the clockwork arm mechanism began.

'I'm not sure we're going back to New Albion any time soon,' proffered Ellen, as much to distract them as to announce any kind of plan. 'We have to find EAR-MOO B and get to the Moon.' She continued, staring into the middle distance out of the hospital room window, not particularly noticing if anyone was listening.

'Heremoowhat?' queried Fitch in a non-too-subtle way. Ellen, however, didn't hear the question as her staring had finally alighted on something that made her jump with excitement.

'Never you mind,' she grinned turning back to them, her arm pointing to something through the window. 'I've just seen how we can do it.' And with that she grabbed her coat and disappeared out of the wardroom.

Two hours later, with Fitch's arm still requiring near constant adjustments from the professor, they found themselves airborne again. In the interregnum, Ellen had snuck onto a local airfield and, erm, borrowed one of the Gaulish ornithopters she had espied from the hospital window. Well when I say "Borrowed" I mean, of course, nicked, but who's going to quibble when the fate of the entire human race was at stake? It was a bit of cramped cockpit, but somehow, they had all squeezed in. This had been achieved by Mrs Tickle being on Ellen's lap, and Professor Lushthorpe, tools in both hands, sitting on Fitch's. Before they had left, Ellen had found, with much arm-waving and gallic confusion, the local rocket-assisted pigeon station and dispatched one of said birds to the war cabinet back in New Albion. The telegram had read: "Location missing EAR-MOO B found, stop. Probably, stop. 40 minutes into Big Caravan Race 20 minutes north, stop. Send cavalry soonest, if not sooner, stop." She would have liked more explanation, but only had 2 Francs on her and it was an extortionate 10 centimes a word. She'd argued at complete cross purposes for nearly 15 minutes as to whether EAR-MOO was one word or two, until the matronly Gallic operator had finally coalesced to the Albionion pilot's point of view and given in. After all, it was nearly lunchtime, and she wasn't going miss her brie and burgundy for the sake of a mere 10 centimes. Ellen just hoped it was enough information for the powers that be to find them. On top of this she was praying that the ornithopter had enough fuel to get them where they needed to be as they flew pretty much dead south, over the Middle-Terranean Sea towards the scorching wastes of the Nubian desert. The flight would have been fairly straightforward had it not became more and more obvious that Fitch's new mechanical arm was a little, well, cantankerous is probably the polite way to say it. Now fully up to, probably, maximum windage, it kept jerking this way and that, occasionally grabbing the controls and trying to divert them to a new course. All the while Lushthorpe muttered to himself and tried to make adjustments with a range of mis-matched tools, but so far it seemed only to have made it worse. This came to a head nearly two hours into their spasmodic flight as all eyes were trained on the desert looking for the giant volcano crater-like pirate base. Another plane, this time a quadplane flying due West, was suddenly on a collision course. The arm on this occasion, almost helpfully, chose to grab the joystick and send them into a somersault. They all yelled as the 'thopter flipped over and they waved lamely at the simian pilot of the Quadplane who shook a fist at them in annoyance. By this point even Ellen could not recover control of the contraption and it seemed they were desert bound. The rest of the adventure would have to be on foot, and for this they were ill-prepared.

'Bracing positions!' warned Ellen, somewhat superfluously, as she noticed that the quadplane they had so nearly come to blows with, appeared to also be crashing not too far from them.

After a less than comfortable crash landing, the second in only three days, they were all mightily relieved to find that no additional limbs had been lost. Although Fitch secretly wished that his new mechanical arm might have been irrevocably damaged by the impact, no such fortune came his way. It was apparent to them all that a new, emergency plan was needed and quickly, and the best that any of them could come up with was getting a fire going that at least might attract attention of some sort. So, this they did, although mostly with bits of their own clothing and parts of the mangled ornithopter as other kindling was sparse on the ground, it being a desert and all.

It was whilst attempting to get this fire going, with the slightly over the top method of using Fitch's plasma rifle, that they first noticed movement amongst the distant dunes. Looking more keenly they began to see, with increasing alarm, a mass of figures advancing cautiously towards them through the heat haze. Their clothing was coloured perfectly to blend in with the sand and rocks. Swarthy headdresses about their heads and they were brandishing a range of mean looking rifles and pistols.

'Stay behind me!' ordered Fitch, but his mechanical arm had other ideas and gave the approaching strangers a cheery wave. 'Stop that,' Fitch hissed at his limb, but it showed no sign of complying.

'Oh dear,' muttered Lushthorpe, 'another thing to look at.' Fitch ignored him and tried to get his plasma rifle into a position ready to fire with his left hand. Before he could though one of the camouflaged troops popped out of the sand almost right in front of them, his rifle pointing straight at Fitch's head.

'What HO!' the man hollered, 'stay still or ONE will be forced fire. No one wants that, least of all ME. Wot WOT!'

'Smeggy!' cried Lushthorpe peering out from behind Fitch's bulk.

'The VERY same,' cried the man, pulling his headscarf down to reveal a moustachioed face topped with a khaki cap bearing a distinctive gecko and hamster cap badge. 'Captain Panfold Smegerton at YOUR service.' He lowered his weapon and proffered a quivering salute. 'It that you Lushy, you OLD COOT?'

Fitch also lowered his gun and stared at them both with an arched eyebrow.

'Don't worry, this is 'Smeggy Pants' Smegerton, we roomed together at Thornton.'

'Well that's alright then,' muttered Fitch sarcastically. His arm, however, begged to differ and without so much as a "by your leave" it smacked Smeggy Smegerton right across the chops, sending him reeling over the sand.

Fortunately, being a good public school boy, Captain Smegerton of the New Albion Nubian Expeditionary Force (less tongue-twistingly known as either the Desert Geckos or the Fighting Hamsters depending on who you asked) laughed this off then, introductions having been made and since night was tiptoeing closer, instructed his men to set up a bivouac encampment. In the centre of which a most splendid campfire, infinitely superior to their own pathetic attempt, appeared almost out of nowhere. They all sat down to enjoy a well-earned meal and the captain launched into a very loud explanation of how he and his men came to be there.

'Conducting LONG RANGE exercises, DONTCHA know!' he bellowed as the rest of his camouflaged platoon continued to appear from all around to assist with the camp making. 'Good BUNCH this, but absolute PLEBS when it comes to the sandy stuff, FAH FAH. Thought I'd show THEM THE ROPES, teach them to brush behind their TEETH if you follow me, GEFFUFAH!' It had to be said that they didn't really follow him but trying to be polite they nodded along anyway. 'Funny THING though, came across another downed KITE just before yours. Rescued a similar motley CREW. Perhaps even a shade motlier, HA, a ha HA.' He guffawed randomly in the way that only upper class ex-public schoolboy army twits can.

'Ah yes, we nearly hit them,' admitted Ellen, hoping to get on to the topic of pirate bases before too long. 'Are you here because of my pigeon?'

'WHAT PIGEON?' bellowed Smegerton, a man whose volume attenuation seemed permanently on the blink. 'No, NO, we were out this way anyway A FAR FAR. So, what ARE you fine lads and LASSES doing so far out in the Nubian wastelands?'

'Weeeell,' started Ellen, taking an enormous breath, 'We stole a Gaulish ornithopter to find a pirate base in the Nubian desert, that's not really a pirate base it's really a top secret alien transporter device that was used to beam commandos to the Moon fifty years ago,' she stopped for the shortest breath possible her arms held up to prevent Smegerton sticking his metaphorical oar in again '...aaand we've got to find some way to get it working again so we can get back up to the Moon and help them, in turn, get the Martians back to Mars or wherever they came from. I mean, I assume it's Mars, them being Martians and all, ha ha... no? Possibly with some sort of brown gas, but ah, who really knows eh?' She finally came up for air and was expecting Smegerton to launch into a riposte of some kind, but instead he was rubbing his chin thoughtfully.

'Pirate LAIR you SAY!' he partially yelled. 'I think I KNOW the place you mean, big round THING, lots of DRUNK people.'

'That's it!' exclaimed Ellen, jumping up. 'Do you know it?'

'I most certainly do AH!' bellowed the Captain, 'we always look in THERE on our long desert sweeps AH... good place for a BEVVY dontcha know?' He slapped his thigh in excitement. 'We can get you there ON THE MORROW. Do you think the PIRATES might know how to return it to WORKING order?'

'I doubt it,' sighed Ellen, 'it was a long time ago and there's no one there now that remembers those days, as far as I know.'

'Well now I might be able to help there,' came a dreary, boring voice as a new, hunched and bedraggled figure slunk up to their fireside group. They all looked up at the rat-faced man, and Ellen and Fitch gasped in unison as they recognized the rodent-a-like features.

'Snook!' they cried in unison.

'It's Sneer now' replied the dreary voice. 'And Sneer has a brother to avenge!'

To be further continued

XIX

A Martian Calls

[This is an extract from the autobiography of Theodore Pilkington-Rhubarb, chief announcer for the Albion Radiophonic Corporation Light Programme: *Towards the Light or How I Redefined Radio for The Modern Era.*]

"This is New Albion calling, New Albion calling. Good evening, my name is Theodore Pilkington-Rhubarb and you are listening to the ARC Light Programme."

Ah, how those words seem etched into the very fabric of all of our consciousnesses now, but, in truth, the path from slobbering boyhood to radio infamy [*note to editor, is this the word I'm after? Ed: No. Please remember to delete this before going to print.*] 'twas not as smooth as it might appear. It was not for lack of determination however, as I had always known that the airwaves were my destiny. From early moments I had bored my poor Mumsie silly with radiophonic carry-ons using her cheese grater suspended from a metal coat hanger by a pair of old stockings as a microphone. Which reminds me, I really must publish the blue-prints for my fabled suspendered-cheese-o-phone, although I'm not sure how much the youth are entertained by such simple pleasures these days. I digress. Despite this resolute knowledge of where my future lay, the path to the summit of broadcast light entertainment announcing was decidedly wobblier than it ought to have been. Indeed, Mumsie had pushed me initially, for no reason that I can fathom except, perhaps, that she was trying to get rid of me, to try for the priesthood. Not wanting to disappoint my dearest mother I duly applied only to be informed, in no uncertain terms, that belief in an eternal all-knowing deity was actually necessary to enter the Seminary. Well this was certainly news to me. Our own family priest was an atheist of the highest order, indeed he was only finally "convinced" to surrender the frock, when the fact that he'd been embezzling the local parish and frittering all the collection money away by betting on the dogs was proven in court. Hilarious for sure, although hardly holy. Spurned thus I attempted to apply to the Albion Radiophonic Corporation for the first time, only to be told by the then controller, Lord Barking Fruitcake, that he considered me "too short for radio". I trudged home that night thoroughly dejected to discover that, in the meantime, my dear Mumsie had enrolled me in the Navy as she had determined that I should have, what she liked to call, "any old job".

In the end though, the joke was on her, as it turned out I was entirely unsuitable for life afloat and was promptly frogmarched back ashore, where I finally found an eminently suitable role operating the Alarm Repeating System for Macaroni Telegraph™ in shore-to-ship communications. As an aside, you may be interested to know that it was in this very position that I first met Mabel, my ever so slightly over eager assistant, then a Sea Cadet specialising in semaphore stitching and flag ironing. It turned out she was also a dab hand with a pneumatic steam-driven soldering iron, a skill that has rescued me on many an occasion I can tell you. No indeed, I was never happier than when I had a good ARS-MT throbbing in front of me, and my flair with the tippy-tapping of the enciphering keys was legendary in many a sailor's tavern. Oh, they would say, that man can certainly encode an all-points weather report, featuring a force 4.2 gale improving gradually to the west, in a way that brings a smirk to even the hardiest salty tar's chapped lips. Or something like that anyway. Unfortunately, a mere three months into my placement the Royal Albion Navy was accidentally disbanded due to an administrative error at the *Ministry of Homeland Defence (and Attack)* and thus finding myself suddenly unemployed, I thought I'd try my arm at another job for the ARC. This time around, despite the flood of seamen applying for any available vacancies and, almost certainly, due to old Lord Fruitcake's retirement, I finally landed a junior radio announcer's role in the Europa Service. This threw at me a myriad of opportunities to prematurely end my career but, somehow, I managed to swerve them all. A particular, I think you would call it – "highlight", was serving as announcer for *Jeopardy in Icing* an international professional cake-decorating championship hosted in the Gaulish capital of patisserie, Chantilly-en-Mer. Despite not speaking a word of Gaulish, and occasionally lacking the depth of vocabulary to describe yet another round of Crème-Albionase be-whippery or layered crêpe-waffle icing-bag endoodling, I somehow muddled through. I must have been doing something right, or at least mildly humorous, as on returning to auntie's bosom I was promptly requested to be the announcer on an experimental new comedy series – The Spoon Show – written and voiced by that notorious nutter Spoke Mulligan. I say requested, but I later heard that they'd offered it to practically everybody else at the corporation, but all of the responses received were unprintable even on these humble pages. Still, I choose to believe it was my baking banter that tipped the wink in my direction rather than mass rejection by every other employee at the ARC, but who can really say? It turned out to be something that I barely understood, however Mabel, by now my trusty engineer and girl-fix-it, *abso-bloody-lutely* loved it, so I persevered. I like to think that my straight-as-a-die ex-naval-telegraphist meets pastry-decoration-expounder approach added a certain levelling element to what, to my ears at least, was barely organised buffoonery. The show itself, much to my bafflement, was almost universally critically acclaimed and this meant that kudos was acquired by all who had managed to somehow cling on to the careering carousel that emerged from Mulligan's mind. Including yours truly. Fearing somewhat for my sanity, I had been keen in any case to move on to fresher pastures, and this in turn lead to finally landing, what seemed me at least, to be the plum role of chief announcer for the Light Programme. And so, with Mabel in tow I set off for the Metropolis to begin the next chapter in my mastery of the New Albion airwaves. It should also be said that my consummate knowledge, via The Spoon Show of, what was to become known as, "anarchic comedy" held me in good sway when I found myself embroiled in one of the more infamous events to befall the ARC studios, a little adventure that I have named "A Martian Calls" which, if you will indulge me a little further, I will relate to you now.

It had started like any other day at the studio. A myriad of meetings, and meetings about meetings: pre-scripting this, un-de-organising that. All pretty much run o' the mill corporate stuff which gave no clue as to the momentous events that were to follow. Keith Urban-Trousers was being his usual insufferable bore in the pre-production pontification, holding forth on why his show, the preposterously over-named "Luigi Englebert's Rhapsody On Wax" (why he couldn't use his real name I really couldn't tell you, although I have my suspicions) should be moved to the more lucrative, and from Urban-Trousers' point of view personally advantageous, Lady's Gin-Time slot at 1700 hours. Mabel had laughed so hard at this suggestion that she'd spat her mouthful of Darjeeling all over the

Deputy Controller's twinset and she, in turn, had to rule that we were all out of order and, thankfully, the motion was defeated. My own contribution to the conflab, on that - as it turned out - fateful day was even less salubrious (if you can comprehend such a thing) as the only point of order I advanced concerned the questions for the new-fangled Listener's Telephone In Quiz – *Can You Guess What It Is That I'm Describing?* By way of another aside I should explain that the quiz works thus: I have to ask the listener (should one actually deign to telephone the show, we've not been that successful in regards to that, but the less said about that situation the better) three rhyming clues to enable them to guess what it is that I'm describing. If they succeed in this, near-pointless, endeavour on first time of asking they will win three shillings. After that both the returns, and any attempt at retaining a little dignity, diminish rapidly. This segment of the Light Programme had been introduced initially for two reasons, firstly because it was felt that the ratings were a little on the low side (something I dispute, the court case is pending) and nextly because the ARC had invested the sum of 34 pounds, nine shillings and sixpence in a new telephony system and the powers that be felt we ought to "bloody well use it for something". Anyway, I barely recall what the issues with the questions were that day, subsequent events having driven them from my memory, but we conversed, and in the end, it was deemed that the Deputy Controller was right and everyone else was wrong. Même vieux en croute pedant la guerre, or some such. Procedural shenanigans done and dusted, I retired to the staff canteen, via and indeed post-via the bar, for a little repast, and a modest bottle of port, before my traditional pre-show nap on the announcer's settee.

Now dear listener, I mean reader, or perhaps, listener / reader, it should be pointed out that my entire career has been in the flimsier end of lightest of light entertainment and keeping abreast with current affairs was not really my forte. Despite this, it seems that by accident, design or, indeed, innate comic timing, my role in the ensuing events were of some small benefit to the Homeland. Following my nap, I settled myself into the near soporific routine of the Light Programme. The usual introduction, the same old spiel of near desperate hope for a listener to telephone the studio. Urban-Trousers lounging against the console behind the glass screen, attempting to flirt, once again, with Mabel. I tut beneath my breath, and then... the telephone begins to ring. I seize the earpiece a little too hastily, but just in time I remember my old drama teacher's words to calm my impetuousness: "stop fiddling with yourself in your pocket and relax your panting." So, in the end the words come lightly to me,

"Ahoy, 'hoy.   This is the Albion Radiophonic Corporation, Theodore speaking. Good day to you, fair listener, are you prepared to play Can You Guess What It Is That I'm Describing?" At first there is no reply, only a little static on the line. But just as I was about to enquire again, there is a cacophony of unintelligible gobbledygook that, I am ashamed to say, leads me to utter under my breath, "oh here we go again". Then finally the campest metallic voice I have ever heard in all my days, intones the following:

"Dirt grubber of a smelly disposition, this voice represents *Egor the Almost Indestructible*, surrender your strategically vital radiophonic frippery or face grotty death of an irksome nature".

"Mother, is that you?" I replied, as yet not fully seizing weight of the occasion (and having been fooled once too often before). Ordinarily my primary assumption would have been that it was Urban-Trousers, had I not known he was in the control booth behind me.   Another flood of incoherent babble followed and then the crackling voice returned:

"No, Egor is not the bosom of your weaning. He flaps his eyestalks in indignation." I was still none-the-wiser, but being a radio stalwart of, what I felt to be, the highest possible level of professionalism I vamped valiantly.

"Ah, many apologies dearest listener Eager, but you do sound a bit like my mother. Now then, are you ready to play *Can You Guess*

What It Is That I'm Describing?" More vociferous unintelligible shouting came, which caused me to move the earpiece a distance from my ear. Then, as if translating the garble, there followed the robotic voice again,

"You are a petty dropping on the lowest flapping dinosaur dung heap, what is this you chirp of like some insignificant bird with both dull plumage and no intrinsic observation value?"

"Well now," I began, feeling on a firmer footing despite what sounded, almost certainly, like a personal smear, "It works thus, I will give you three clues, and if you are predisposed to solve my riddle with the first proposition, you will win three shillings." (At this point in the telling dearest reader, I will dispense with a description of the incomprehensible foreign-sounding shouting and relay only the Albionesque responses, otherwise we shall surely be here a fortnight.)

"Cretinous edifice of dirt-begrubbing insects, cease your infantile gurgling and acquiesce to Egor's offer of, reasonablish, ultimatitude."

"I'll take that as a yes then," I offered, not really understanding one syllable and, by this point, believing in the very depths of my mortal soul that I was being pranked anyway. One does what one needs to do to preserve what little is left of one's dignity in such situations. At least, that's what I told myself, in any case I'd been so ground down by the lack of focus by previous callers that I was on a mission to get on with the rest of the programme anyway.

"Very well, here is the first clue for three shillings." I cleared my throat melodramatically. It's a thing I like to do. Mumsie says it's me over-egging my pudding, but you know what, I like my desserts with a surfeit of ovoids, so sue me. Without any kind of detectable "on air" interruption, I found that day's Listener's Quiz questions and, chest puffed out, read the first clue confidently: "Fleet of air I be, you can't even begin to see me." Given that in this book I am trying to present a true picture of the evening's events, I must confess that at this point I turned to give Mabel one of my hardest of hard stares, since the question was somewhat sub-optimal of even the lowest standards that we have tried to maintain in our radio endeavours. It was at this point that I noticed that Mabel and Urban-Trousers were pressed up against the studio door attempting, it seemed, to prevent someone's ingress to the control booth. Now unsurprisingly this was somewhat distracting, but ever the consummate professional, I attended to matters on the telephone without so much as a hesitation, repetition, deviation or, I like to think, repetition.

"Erm, er, no no, not that, erm so for one shilling and tuppence, oer, no thruppence, here is the third, no wait I mean second clue. Ahem." I took a deep breath and prayed for some semblance of sanity to return. "Sometimes I do pong, but never for too long. Oh, for heaven's sake Mabel," this last bit I uttered under my breath so as it should not be broadcast to the nation, "this really is the worst set of clues yet!" Mabel and Urban-Trousers were still engaged in their energetic door-jamming hi-jinks, for which, as yet, I had no explanation, so there was really no option except to wade further into this cesspit of ineptitude with all limbs akimbo. "I don't suppose you have an answer caller? I'd really like to crack on if it's all the same to you?" There came at this point the sound of what could only be described as a physical struggle down the line, and perhaps even a gunshot, which was mildly alarming. Still I'd been in far more challenging situations on a night out with some of my Navy chums, so it didn't really put me off my stride, well not too much anyway. Finally, after some further unintelligible ranting, the listener, Eager, did offer a reply,

"Buckets of insatiable desire to occupy your radiophonic control base drench me in saliva earth piglet, who is worth less than a flea!" I checked the paper carefully, just in case I'd misread the question and this caller was cleverer than I had given him credit. But alas, it just wasn't the right answer.

"No, no that's not it. Far simpler really, I get the feeling you are trying too hard." I attempted to sound encouraging, yet impatient.

"Egor is trying hard beyond the hardness of a hard-armoured war chariot with extra armour on three sides, oh slimy mucus trail of a retarded shell-less snail," came the reply.

"Well I can't knock your effort," I retorted, more generously than I felt, "but if we can take the personal insults down a notch, I'd be grateful." I was answered by only more gurgling and snorting, so took this as a sign to wrap things up. "Very well, for tuppence ha-penny. Here is your final clue. Grab me you cannet (sic), although I do make up some planet (also sic)." I was beyond disgust with the quality of the material I was being forced to work with, so didn't even bother to see if Mabel was registering my displeasure with proceedings. The line crackled again, and the camp voice returned, sounding fairly unflustered by the sheer volume of cacophony audible on all sides of the situation.

"Dirt stain of exceptional worthlessness, Egor offers you this final chance at surrendership. Offer up your seat of communication enthronement or prepare for a fate worse than insufferable hardship at the hands of a grumpy belligerent!" It seemed by this point the caller had resorted to blatant aggression win me over, but since I'd been called far worse in team-building exercises I was not moved to give in. In any case, with the studio clock ticking on towards story time, this player had reached the end of his tether, and so, quite frankly, had I.

"No that's not it! That's nothing to do with it!" I exclaimed louder than I should have and, feeling the burden of the second hand ticking closer to the hour, I must confess I bypassed my usual urbane professionalship and strayed into the realms of surliness. "The answer is gas." There was a sound not unlike a raspberry being blown down the line, and I'm afraid my cool finally exploded into unmitigated annoyance, "Gas! Gas! Gas!" I hollered into the mouthpiece. With this there was an unedifying scream which was followed by the camp metallic voice offering a plaintive "Oh mummy not that brown emanation again!" after which the line went dead.

"How rude," I muttered as I hung up the earpiece, and with that, it was indeed time for the next segment of the show. "And now it's time for, Slumbertime Stories..." I began; however, my soliloquy was cut short as Mabel entered the studio, arms flailing and screaming at the top of her lungs.

"The Martians are here! We have to go now!"

"Go, go where?" I enquired, worrying that we were still on air, although by this point it turned out my microphone had actually been dead for the previous ten minutes and the emergency broadcast spiral wax-o-graph was being aired in my place, warning all citizens to stay calm and run like the devil himself for the countryside. And without so much as a "goodnight dear listener I wish you dreams of a bright future", we did likewise.

Now, it turns out, much after all this carry on had subsided, that the Martian – Egor - had been so overwhelmed by my screaming about gas at him, that he had abandoned his attack on the studio and retreated to the safety of one of his tripods to cower like a cowardly custard. Allowing New Albion troops and the ARC staff to render the radio station inoperable and move to our emergency bunker, at a top-secret location, to continue broadcasting. Somewhat inadvertently I had actually enabled the whole retreat to be successfully concluded with Mabel's rather underwhelming quiz questions. Quite what troubled them so much about the threat of gas, one can only guess. But it saved both the day and, rather more importantly, my career. One can only muse on what the turn of events would have been, had that week's quiz been the one about the goat! I truly dread to think. Still fate is not what we do, but what is dumped upon us, and with that I must conclude this chapter and, indeed this volume of my memoirs. Life must now intervene, and another set of stories be acquired, for future publication. One can only wonder what on earth, or indeed off earth, might come next.

XX

EAR-MOO B

The journey to the dilapidated pirate base in the desert was not as arduous as it might have been due to Captain Panfold "Smeggy-pants" Smegerton's rather well co-ordinated New Albion Nubian Expeditionary Force. These crack troops turned out to be rather more adept at desert manoeuvres than Smegerton had previously given them credit and the Desert Hamsters, or Fighting Geckos, depending on whom you asked, even managed to whistle up some camels. They also gathered up the spacesuits and any other useful looking equipment from the downed ornithopter and squirreled, or should that be hamstered, it away somewhere in their baggage train. Alongside the camels they also had a couple of desert haulers with large rubber wheels, an armoured car and a staff car in various states of roadworthiness. Sir Lushthorpe, Mrs. Tickle and Ellen Hall managed to bag seats in the staff car; Rusty, Sneer and Belistranka were found space in a sandhauler, behind which their, still airworthy, quadplane was attached. This left Fitch, and his cantankerous arm, to ride an equally, if not slightly more, cantankerous dromedary. Fortunately said creature was too stubborn to be put off by the arm's attempting to signal right turn at every opportunity. Fitch, equally stubbornly, even managed to doze off for a little while.

Their arrival after some five hours of transit was greeted by the pirates with an unexpected degree of relish. It seemed that, true to his word, Smegerton was popular with these rogues and almost immediately bottles of contraband were produced to toast their arrival. Ellen, however, tried hard to avoid making eye contact with the Pirate Queen, just on the slim off-chance that she might be recognised as the one who shut her in *the sink* and sent all her warhorses charging off into the sand, the last time she was here. Fortunately, it seemed the Pirate Queen had no such recollection of the misdemeanour and the only interaction was to be offered a cheery hug and a goblet of brandy, or similar. It soon became clear, however, that their main purpose – of reviving EAR-MOO B – was being somewhat subsumed in the bonhomie and was in danger of being drunk under the table before really managing to get its elbows on the bar. Noting that Lushthorpe and Sneer were off to one side gazing at the ruined, and sand covered, gantries and machinery, scratching their heads, Ellen tried to sidle out of the revelries and join them. However, she found her way blocked by a teenage girl, who looked at her with wide, brown eyes, head tipped on one side, in a way that was all too familiar.

'Oh, hello there,' offered Ellen, trying to be cheerful, yet keen to move on.

'Hello,' replied the girl eyeing her increasingly quizzically, 'I'm Simone and I'm thirteen and three quarters.'

'How lovely,' replied Ellen, beginning to feel a little anxious that the girl might recognise her and relay her identity to the Pirate Queen. This could really put a harpoon in the iron warhorse leg, almost literally.

'Do I know you from somewhere?' enquired the girl, a frown beginning to crease her forehead.

'Nope, no sirree, definitely never been here, or seen you before...' stuttered Ellen who, as a general rule, found it almost impossible to lie, and was feeling her face redden by the second. 'Anyway, no time to talk I have to help these gentlemen get your base thingy working again. Bye for now,' and with that she strode confidently off towards the inventors, hoping this would placate the girl. However, she was not easily put off and began to follow after her.

'No, I'm really sure I know you from somewhere. Don't you have a dark-haired friend?'

'No, nope, no friends at all actually. I make a point of being very unfriendly,' garbled Ellen, reddening further and walking even quicker to try and shake her off.

'Ellen!' called Fitch, rather unhelpfully, from somewhere behind them, causing them both to turn around to see the tall mercenary stomping towards them. 'Is this girl bothering you?'

'Ellen!' snapped the girl excitedly, whirling to look back at the red-faced pilot. But rather than getting angry and alerting the other pirates, she instead clapped her hands excitedly and jumped up and down with what gave every appearance of being glee. 'Oh, you came back, you came back. I knew you would! Wait till I tell mummy!'

'I'd really rather you didn't,' exclaimed Ellen, making frantic motions with her hands to shush her. 'I'm not sure she'd be very happy with me.'

'Oh nonsense,' admonished Simone. 'She thought it was all highly exciting, best thing that's happened for ages.' By this point, and panting slightly, Fitch had caught up with them both, his mechanical arm waving the Martian plasma gun around somewhat wildly.

'Do you need me to incapacitate her?' he wheezed through panting breaths. The ladies both looked at him wide-eyed, and Ellen held up her arms to prevent him taking any violent action.

'No, no it's fine Fitch, I think everything is okay.'

'It's more than okay,' exclaimed Simone, 'this is the best day ever.' And with that she leant forward and gave Ellen the second biggest hug she'd ever experienced. Relieved and seeing Fitch, and his clockwork arm, stand down, Ellen returned the hug, and for a few moments she recalled the last time she'd shared a hug with another dark-skinned woman. 'I really must tell mummy you're here,' continued Simone, not noticing the small tear in the corner of Ellen's eye. 'She knows you're my total hero. I even named my boat after you.'

'Boat! In the desert?' growled Fitch, but before he could guffaw further, Ellen held a finger to her lips. Fortunately, he had the sense to pipe down.

'It's a long story, but this girl's always wanted to be a sailor, if I recall correctly.' Simone smiled in return and seemed rather overcome with emotion herself. She turned as if to head back to the other pirates, but Ellen caught her arm. 'Wait just a bit, won't you?' she asked the girl. 'I really need to speak with my friends about getting this, er thing, working again.' She swept her arm to indicate the crater-like ring of sand-covered contraptions all around them, which Lushthorpe and Sneer were also eyeballing with increasing despair. In fact, at this point, Lushthorpe, who was prone to outbursts of wailing despair, let out a 'Oh we'll never get this pile of crap working in a month of Sundays!'

Ellen turned back to the girl, with a shrug intended to convey "see what I have to put up with". The girl appeared to be ready to acknowledge this, but her eyes still gleamed with excitement, albeit mildly abated.

'You *will* come and see my boat?' she pleaded.

'Of course, we just have to come up with some sort of plan to fix the EAR-MOO, and it's not exactly got off to a good start.' She turned to go, hoping that the girl might finally leave them to it. However, something Ellen had said seemed to have caused her to furrow her brow once again.

'EAR-MOO?' she asked.

'Yes dear,' interjected Lushthorpe, in only a mildly patronising way as he joined the group. 'It's going to take all my many, many years of quite brilliant engineering brilliance to understand how to get this contraption anywhere near working again.' He gave out another wail and clutched his head in exasperation.

'EAR-MOO?' repeated Simone, shaking her head in a typically teenage way.

'Yes dear. EAR-MOO, it stands for Earth to Moo...' Simone cut her off with a sharp wave of her slender arm.

'I know what EAR-MOO stands for, thank you very much,' she muttered with teenage petulance, her eyes wide with indignation.

'Good, good,' interjected Ellen stepping in before Simone went full pirate child on Lushthorpe's rear-end. 'Perhaps you can help us with all this? I was hoping someone could.' This seemed to placate Simone a little, but she was still clearly put out. She folded her arms in continued annoyance.

'I'm sure we really don't need this little girl's help,' added Lushthorpe, very unhelpfully. 'We are going to need tools and engineers and years, and years of experience to even start on this thing.' He swept his arm to indicate the sheer scale of the ruins, and hence the task ahead. But Simone was having none of it.

'Well if you actually listen to me for a minute, then I'd be able to tell you that this thing...' she swept her arm obviously mocking Lushthorpe's melodramatics. He looked ready to explode, but before he could she continued, '... isn't the EAR-MOO at all!' With this pronouncement Lushthorpe's eyes nearly popped out of his head, and Fitch was heard to offer a non-too-subtle 'Ha!' barely under his breath.

Ellen grabbed Simone with both arms,

'What did you just say?'

'This,' she swept her eyes this time, as Ellen was pinning her arms to her side, 'isn't the EAR-MOO – it's just a decoy to make everyone think it's out of action.'

'Well if this isn't the transporter, where is it?' spluttered Lushthorpe utterly furious that some mere teenager knew more than him.

'Well,' Simone started, glad to be getting one over on the pompous man. 'If you are nice to me, I might just show you.'

'Oh Simone, don't listen to him, he's just having a bad week.' Chortled Ellen, hoping that this would placate the girl. 'Show us where the EAR-MOO is and then I promise I'll come and look at your boat.' The girl looked at Lushthorpe, who had the sense to bite his tongue, at Ellen, at Lushthorpe and back at Ellen again before a smile finally crept over her face.

'Oh goody, you're going to love it,' she gave Ellen another bear hug. 'The boat that is, the other thing is boring.' She added for Lushthorpe's benefit, and it seemed that the deal was sealed.

So, led by Simone, the little gang of Ellen, Fitch, Lushthorpe, Mrs. Tickle and the snivelling Sneer, made their way amongst the wreckage and sand dunes of the pirate lair until they came to a big, roughly circular, pile of sand. Here Simone brought them to a halt, and without much enthusiasm announced. 'Here it is, now who wants to see my boat?'

'I don't see it,' sneered Sneer in his rat like voice however, his tones were so dull that no one seemed to hear him.

'I don't see it!' wailed Lushthorpe whom it was impossible not to hear.

'I just said that,' murmured Sneer, but again no one seemed to notice.

'It's underneath silly,' tutted Simone. 'Give me a hand.' And with that she found the edge of a tarpaulin and began to pull it up. Fitch and Ellen stepped forward to help, and it turned out that what they thought was a mound of sand was actually only a light coating of sand on canvas and, as they pulled on the sheets, they came away fairly easily to reveal shining equipment underneath. With some effort, after ten minutes or so the whole edifice was revealed. There was a lot of complicated looking machinery, dials, pipes, a couple of brass telescopes, valves and wires all in reasonably good order considering they were at least half a century old. In the centre of it all was a circle of exotic looking shimmering material, however it's diminutive size, roughly six feet in diameter, caused Lushthorpe to look rather worried.

'It's rather small isn't it?' he moaned. At this Simone looked rather offended.

'Yes, I suppose I'd imagined it bigger,' conceded Ellen, 'but at least it looks like it might work, if only we knew how.'

'I know how,' muttered a dull voice, however no one seemed to hear.

'Looks pretty complicated,' growled Fitch looking at the nearest baroque control panel.

'It's easy enough, if you know how,' came the dull muttering again.

'Fiendishly difficult!' wailed Lushthorpe, also examining some of the contraptions.

'It really isn't,' came a rat-like voice.

'Well I've no idea,' chipped in Ellen, 'you've seen it operate Fitch, any clues were to start?'

'I know where to start,' came the unremarkable, sneery voice again.

'Not a chuffing clue,' growled Fitch, 'I was rather pre-occupied last time I saw one of these. I thought our scientist friend here, was supposed to be good at this stuff.'

'I know how it works!' muttered Sneer once again in his utterly morbid tones.

'Well I'm sure if I can disassemble it to its bare components and make some notes...' started Lushthorpe, sounding close to utter exasperation.

'There's really no need,' sneered Sneer managing to sound both dull and vexed at the same time.

'Not sure we've got time for this!' interjected Ellen. At this point Mrs Tickle also offered her tuppence ha-penny with a loud meow and pointed one paw up into the sky, where the Moon was indeed visible.

'Ah the moon is nigh, we'll never get it dissembled, examined, documented and reassembled in time!' wailed Lushthorpe with utter despondency. 'We must start dismantling it now, destructively if necessary!'

'Now you're talking,' approved Fitch, readying his plasma rifle.

'No really, don't do that!' semi-exclaimed Sneer, who by this time was looking at them all, wondering why they didn't seem to be acknowledging him.

'Ah it will take too long!' chipped in Ellen, beginning to sound flustered.

'I KNOW HOW TO WORK IT!' yelled Sneer as loud as he could possibly manage. Which wasn't very loud, and was certainly still very monotonous, but it was enough to cause everyone else present to jump, having not realising that he was even there.

'Where did you come from?' demanded Fitch.

'I've been here all the time, why can't you hear me?'

'Sorry Sneer, we had no idea you were still with us,' added Ellen, also surprised, but realising that he was probably their only hope.

'Does anyone want to see my boat now?' chirped Simone.

'NOT NOW!' replied everyone, including Sneer, and they began to argue loudly amongst themselves.

'Well there's gratitude!' huffed Simone, folding her arms again. At this point in the debacle, Mrs. Tickle jumped up into Ellen's arms and meowed loudly a second time. This seemed to break the air of acrimony and Ellen realised that it was time for someone to take control, and that someone was pretty much going to have to be her. She held up an arm for quiet, and when it was finally acknowledged she laid out the plan as she saw it.

'Right, Sneer, Snook, whatever your name is, and wherever you just appeared from, show Sir Grenville how to work the contraption.' Before Lushthorpe could react, she added 'Sir Grenville, we need you to then replicate the transmitter on a bigger scale, so your understanding is vitally important to the whole proceeding.' Fortunately, Lushthorpe's ego seemed mollified by this, so she turned to the other man in the ensemble. 'Fitch, we need your military brain to help work out what to send up and in what order, considering that we've only got pi r squared of about three feet to play with.' Fitch looked confused by the maths initially, but soon twigged what she was on about, so nodded his agreement. 'Oh, and we need to find our spacesuits and anything else here to make more as, presumably, we're going to be arriving in vacuum.'

'And what will you be doing?' enquired Lushthorpe, only half interested, as Sneer was already beginning to pore over the controls and didn't want to miss anything vital.

'Oh, Mrs Tickle and I have a very important mission,'

'And what's that?' asked Simone, who was still standing with her arms folded.

'We're going to look at a boat,' chortled Ellen with a little wink. The smile that came over Simone's face was certainly something to behold.

Unfortunately, their general smugness at having come up with a half decent plan was interrupted by the arrival on the scene of

Captain Smegerton, clearly half cut, and therefore even more randomly vari-loud than usual.

'Sorry to INTERRUPT!,' he semi-bellowed, 'but MY chaps have OBSERVED some UNIDENTIFIED wallahs approaching rapido from the EAST AND the west AND THE EAST hah! Thought IT best I got all HANDS on the DECK. A FAH FAHFAH.'

'Oh goodness,' muttered Ellen trying to take in this news, 'everyone continues with what needs doing for now, we only have a couple of hours before we lose the Moon.'

'I can think and fight,' offered Fitch.

'Let's hope that's not necessary, it might be the cavalry after all.'

'From two directions?'

'Well we'll find out, won't we?' And with that Ellen, Fitch and Mrs. Tickle made off after the, slightly swaying, Smegerton to see who or what was on its way to join them.

At the far end of the compound, near where the Pirate's dingy living quarters were located was a watchtower, that had clearly seen better days. This was where they all headed whilst Desert Hamsters and pirates scuttled all around them, with varying levels of inebriation, to take up defensive positions.

Fitch, with Ellen right on his elbow was first to the top of the tower and his arm took the binoculars from one of Smegerton's troop without really asking. Still none of them, seasoned troops that they were, seemed keen argue to argue with a 6' 8" battle-scarred gentleman with a mechanical arm. And they were wise not to.

Fitch scanned both east and then west for a good minute in each direction, before handing the binoculars on to Ellen.

'Well I'm no great expert,' he started, 'but I would say that eastwards is a bizarre collection of exotic contraptions, the like of which I have never seen in all my days proceeding with undue haste, that could be deemed aggressive, towards our position in determined fashion.' Ellen gulped taking in this intimidating scenario.

'And to the west?' she enquired, hardly daring think as she brought the binoculars up to bear, hoping it wouldn't be so bad.

'Martians' stated Fitch with utter certainty. Indeed, he was right on the money. Ellen observed the western approaches first, and it was clearly a collection of tripods and war-wheels, the likes of which she, also, had never seen before. The sight of this made her hands tremble so hard that it was very difficult to bring the binoculars into focus as she swung them around to the east to try and make out the other group. When she eventually got the lenses into focus, she gave out a little whoop.

'What do you see?' asked Fitch, intrigued by her response.

'Oh, something good,' she started.

'Mind sharing?'

'Don't mind at all,' she grinned, handing the eyeglasses back to the Albion sentry. 'La Caravan is coming to our aid.'

'How long do we have until they get here?' babbled Lushthorpe as he busied himself with a control panel that Sneer had deemed safe enough for him to be let loose on.

'The Martians or the caravan?' asked Ellen, who had just arrived with their two of their five intact spacesuits and Mrs Tickle in tow.

'Either, any?!'

'Smegerton seems to think the Martians will be on us in 20 minutes judging by their approach, the caravan may beat them by a head.' But Lushthorpe didn't seem to hear as Sneer called him over to one of the telescopes to explain something arcane. So instead she looked over the array of alien equipment and it seemed, as Sneer had predicated, that all did appear to be in some semblance of working order. At this moment Fitch arrived with the other two human spacesuits, and Mrs. Tickle's smaller suit, plus a collection of weapons he had acquired from somewhere.

'Then we really need to get on with this,' he muttered, dumping the load and sitting down to wipe his brow. 'We need to decide who's going up first, I would suggest we can get two on the transmitter, plus Mrs. Tickle and some armaments.'

'You and me then?' asked Ellen, pulling out her suit and laying her bronze and glass space helmet on a handy bench.

'Yeah, well, about that,' mumbled Fitch, looking slightly abashed. 'Slight problem there, that this thing won't fit in my suit,' he nodded his head to his clockwork arm, which chose that moment to try and randomly swat a fly, although none appeared visible.

'Ah,' was all Ellen could think to reply. 'That's not ideal. I mean, with Mrs Tickle we have someone who can guide us to safety, but I was hoping for someone who knew how to handle a gun at my side.'

'Perhaps I can help with that?' they all turned as a new figure appeared by the EAR-MOO. The stranger had clearly just arrived from the desert, their heavy cotton fatigues grubby with dust, goggles and a scarf wound over and across their caked with sand.

Fitch, erring on the side of caution, brought up a pistol and motioned (approximately) with his metal arm for Ellen to stay back. 'And who might you be exactly?' he growled. The newcomer reached up and lifted the googles so a pair of green eyes set in dark skin with grimy rings around them.

'Oh, I know those eyes!' exclaimed Ellen, pushing past Fitch and moving to hug the stranger. 'Cleanta!' And indeed, it was her. After a brief hug, as time was pressing, Ellen introduced the King's Agent to

Fitch, with whom she managed to shake hands after only three attempts, a new record for the mechanical arm, and the others. Introductions made she moved forward to look over the EAR-MOO which, although seemingly ready, was clearly causing Sneer some issues.

'Missing something?' enquired Cleanta as Lushthorpe also took a break to shake her hand. It was Sneer that replied,

'We appear to be one thermogromitide-compostulator short of a Martian light elevator.' With this Cleanta reached into her canvas bag and brought out a shining object that resembled a small diode valve. Sneer reached out a bony hand to take it without any ceremony, although he was heard to mutter a barely audible 'thanks' under his breath.

'Ah the family heirloom,' winked Ellen to Cleanta as Sneer, slunk over to a silver-fronted cabinet with a triple-tined handle, snapped it open and, carefully, inserted the object into a slot that seemed a perfect fit.

'Something like that,' winked Cleanta back. With this Ellen's heart skipped a beat as the circular disk at the heart of the machine suddenly lit up with a pearlescent glow and a small cloud of steam wafted out of one of the brass tubes connected to the ancillary equipment. Sneer rubbed his hands with what could quite easily have been glee. 'She is ready.' He announced, in his gratingly morose tones. However, there was no time for any celebration as without any warning an arcing line of blue fire howled over their heads and sliced through one of the (fake) disused gantries, bringing it crashed down amongst the figures bustling about the fort. Returning gunfire was heard almost immediately, but Fitch spoke first to keep everyone focussed on the task in hand.

'We are already in range of the Martian's heat rays. Suit up, you need to go!' There was an edge of anxiety in his voice that Ellen had not heard before in any of their previous adventures. 'Sir Grenville, help Mrs Tickle into her suit, and this young lady into

Carshalton's.' Lushthorpe moved with alacrity to assist and even Sneer slunk over to see if he could help. Fitch turned to assist Ellen, who was already moving nimbly to don her heavy-duty cotton and leather suit. At the very last moment, she saw Fitch's picture book and decided she'd rather have it than not, so stuffed it into the front of the suit before fastening it tightly. It wasn't long before they were ready as more gunfire was heard and with a roar, Belistranka's Quadplane roared overhead moving towards the Martian threat.

'You must take the plasma rifle,' muttered Fitch as he glanced in all directions, trying to understand how great the threat was from the approaching tripods. Ellen held her gauntleted hands up clearly refusing the proffered weapon.

'No, your need is greater. Take out the tripods and keep the EAR-MOO safe. We'll need you to join us when you can.' Behind them there went up a great cacophony of whooping and the Pirate Queen and her motley gang could be seen, in full warpaint, mounting their iron horses and preparing to ride out. 'They're a brave bunch,' Ellen brought her hands back down, 'But they need your help here first.' There was a series of pops from near the watch tower as Smegerton's Desert Geckos took this moment to open fire with some small, cast iron mortars.

'You'll need me more, I think,' growled Fitch, but he seemed to concede her point.

'Indeed I will, get Lushthorpe to modify your suit with the arm on the outside and you'll be a great asset. Until then, erm, hold the fort. Literally.' With what was an almost shout from Sneer, it seemed the time for departure had arrived. Fitch though, was not a man of goodbyes. He assisted Ellen with attaching her dome-shaped helmet, and then tapped on it twice with his index finger on the glass. 'Keep your eyes open, and don't forget to duck,' was all he could think of to say. Ellen laughed, steaming up the inside of the helmet briefly. As it cleared, she gave him a big smile.

'Give the Martians hell,' she said, by way of benediction. And with that Fitch nodded and turned to head to the fort wall as all around great crashes of explosions and cannon fire rent the air. Ellen briefly wondered if she would ever see him again, but there was no time to dwell on this thought as Cleanta caught her arm and thrust a large pistol into her hand.

'No idea why they have these here, or how Fitch found them,' crackled Cleanta's dusky voice through the helmet intercom, 'But these guns are designed for use with snow gloves, so we can use them with our gauntlets.' Ellen took the pistol awkwardly and, gathering up Mrs. Tickle III in her dinky spacesuit, she followed Cleanta between a couple of brass pipes, coughing steam and sparks in equal measure, onto the small glowing disk. Her breathing was quickening by the second and fogging up the helmet, but through billowing clouds of smoke she could make out Sneer and Lushthorpe taking turns looking through telescopes and adjusting baroque looking instruments. She tried to calm herself as best she could as she felt the cat fidget in her arms. There was another flash of eerie blue light, and more pops from the mortars, which sounded even more distant now she had her helmet on. There was a radio system between her and Cleanta and, cleverly, Lushthorpe had also taken the system from his suit so he could talk to them.

'Sneer tells me to tell you that we are close to being ready to initiate transit,' came Lushthorpe's voice into her headset. But Ellen felt like she was outside her body somewhere looking in, and the voice sounded oddly distant. Mrs. Tickle was still now, as was Cleanta, just a foot or so away from her. The light from cannon and heat ray fire flickering off her brass helmet and segmented glass vision panels. She seemed to be saying something, but Ellen didn't hear it.

'Optimum operating temperature approaches,' came Lushthorpe's voice crackling in her earpiece, but the words sounded as alien as the glow from the circular floor beneath her. A colossal explosion suddenly came from somewhere behind Ellen and the force of it nearly knocked her over, fortunately Cleanta reacted quickly and held them all upright. A great blanket of dust and sand passed over the EAR-MOO, lit from below by the pearlescent light of the floor disk, which now seemed to be brighter than ever. Without any other warning it also started to heat up, and Ellen felt her body temperature rapidly increase to dangerous levels. Sweat was starting to pour down her face and despite her usual calm nature, she realised she was starting to panic. Mrs. Tickle also twisted in her arms and she had to struggle to hang on to her. Cleanta's arms were there, but neither of them seemed to be totally stable. The obscuring cloud cleared briefly, and she saw Sneer, his rat like features glaring oddly at them his hands raised and giving a cheesy, double thumbs-up. Ellen wanted to scream, but her throat felt dry and the sound was stuck in her mouth. The intercom crackled again, but she didn't hear anyone speak. Perhaps this was all a bad idea. Perhaps someone else should go. Another cloud of smoke enveloped them, the intercom crackled again, but this time a voice Ellen did not recognise, intoned blandly, 'Did you know that light is both a particle and a wave?' The floor glowed bright intense white and became so hot that it was uncomfortable beyond anything Ellen had ever felt. So, is this how it ends? She thought. Sautéed to death on a Martian griddle. The heat continued to rise and the light from the floor grew so intense that even with her eyes screwed shut, all she could see was brilliant white. Just as she felt resigned to death, everything changed. It went from the hottest she'd ever felt to the coldest. From the brightest light to the darkest dark. She shivered hard and was relieved to feel that she was still holding Mrs. Tickle, or whatever was left of her. She opened her eyes. The machinery was the same, Mrs Tickle was in her arms, Cleanta was stood just a foot away from her, but everything else was different. The sky was jet black, the landscape - a crater-covered visage - was a grey powdery juxtaposition to the brass and gold artefacts of the Martian machinery around her. There was no other conclusion to come to. They were on the Moon.

In her natural element at last, Mrs Tickle jumped out of Ellen's trembling arms. Relieved of this weight, Ellen brought up her pistol and looked around trying to comprehend what had just happened and where they now were. Just ahead of her Cleanta was doing the same with slightly more military precision. They were standing on a similar pearlescent disk to the one they had just left behind on the Earth. Arcane and complex equipment surrounded them, but beyond that was grey dust and craters. Ellen felt light, both in body and in head, as though she was in a strange, but not unpleasant dream. Her body was beginning to warm up again as the heating elements in her spacesuit began to glow. Her earpiece crackled and Cleanta's voice, edged with nervousness, rang through,

'Rockets ahead of us, bunkers a way off to the right.' Ellen followed where she was indicating with her pistol. The rockets she could see, although they were an awful long way off, the bunkers she couldn't spot, but a moving figure caused her to jump.

'Cleanta!' was all she could find to say, her throat still raspingly dry.

'Already seen them!' came Cleanta's sharp retort as she crouched and brought her gun to bear, not even really knowing if it would work in the vacuum of the Moon. The figure continued to advance towards them, two others now visible behind. Somewhat to their relief, they were clearly humanoid in shape, with two legs and arms in beyond ancient looking spacesuits. The first figure held up an arm in what, it clearly presumed, was a symbol of peace, although the other arm held a rather nasty looking harpoon gun. Cleanta kept her pistol pointed in the figure's direction whilst indicating with her other arm that they should hold still. They were both relieved that the figure appeared to comply. Ellen continued to stare, praying that the figure was not a foe, and as she did so a cat, she assumed to be Mrs Tickle, came past her right leg and also took up a watchful position. When another cat, in a much older looking spacesuit, also did the same on her left, and then a third appeared behind Cleanta, Ellen gave a little squeal.

'Erm, rather more cats than we started out with!' she squealed through the intercom. Before Cleanta could reply another, male, voice came through her earpiece.

'Stay still please. The cats are just checking if you are human.' Ellen ignored the voice and spun around to see an elderly figure in the oldest looking spacesuit she had seen yet right behind her, with at least four more cats in suits all around them. 'Oh, and I'm Trout by the way, should have said that sooner probably, Erasmus Trout private first-class Albion Expeditionary Force open parenthesis Extra-terrestrial close parenthesis.' He nodded as the cats all seemed satisfied with their examinations. 'Thank you for coming and bringing Mrs Tickle back safely.' The man came up alongside them and it seemed pretty clear they were on the same side, Mrs Tickle being the intermediary, and the fact their spacesuits worked on the same radio frequency. Cleanta nodded in response, and despite herself Ellen managed to extend a hand in greeting, although at this moment all she was thinking of was getting this suit off and having a nice hot bath.

'Glad you managed to get EAR-MOO B working I should add,' continued the man. 'Are there any others here?'

'Nope, no siree, just the two of us. Oh, and Tickle of course.'

'Of course,' growled Trout as the other man, presumably his comrade, joined them, lowering his weapon as he arrived. 'Just two you say, well it's a start I suppose.'

'Yes, sorry about that, spot of bother back on the, erm, Earth, y'know. More should follow. Erm, hopefully.'

'Well you'll do for starters,' added Trout, realising he had probably not sounded grateful enough. Before he could add anything to seem more thankful however, a cry went up over the airwaves: 'Tripod!' and all eyes turned to see the three-legged craft picking its way around a distant crater. At this point the elderly Albion troopers and space cats moved with, steady, but resolute purpose. More suited figures appeared and a great canvas screen was hauled up around the EAR-MOO and all were ushered towards a, previously hidden, steel hatchway nearby. 'Get underground,' came the instruction with which they all complied, moving in the lopping run required by the Moon's gravity, to the safety of the bunker. The cats nipping in just at the last minute before the airlock was sealed.

Once all was secured at the airlock, with observers appointed to look for more EAR-MOO arrivals, Trout removed his helmet and then helped Ellen and Cleanta with theirs. His visage was that of an elderly statesman, close cropped hair and slim, but jowly, jaw. After securing the helmets he reached for a pair of spectacles and put them on. Then he led them further into the secret complex to an area where they could sit and take stock. All around them a multitude of cats looked on with as much interest, if not more, than the geriatric Albion soldiers. Further introductions were in order as Trout gave instructions for water and food to be brought.

'This is "Chatty" Chattenborough, he doesn't say much,' explained Trout indicating the man on his left, 'and this is Flashman.' A nod to the darker skinned gentleman to his right. 'We've sent for Corporal Longstocking. Sergeant Rogers is really in charge, but he's somewhat indisposed right now.' Ellen nodded to each in turn.

'I'm Ellen and this is Cleanta, sorry it's taken so long to get to you. Do you have a plan for defeating the Martians?' she asked, more in hope than certainty.

'Well, I suppose we were rather hoping you would have one,' responded Flashman, suppressing note of dismay in his voice, although not really enough to unnoticeable.

'Erm, yes, well sorry about that too,' muttered Ellen, feeling her face redden a little. 'I guess we thought you might remember how it was done last time around, since you were, y'know, involved and all.' She tried to sound as non-judgemental as she could, however it was Trout's turn to sound embarrassed.

'Well quite. Trouble is we don't seem to be able to remember. We are getting on a bit it's true, but the memories of how it was done seem to have escaped us, one and all.' At this point a rotund figure hobbled into the room, bearing glasses of clear liquid, which were excepted with relish by Ellen and Cleanta. This gave a few moments for thought and in that time, Ellen remembered Fitch's book.

'Perhaps this might jog your memory?' she offered, pulling the battered picture book from her spacesuit. 'It's just a children's book, but it seems to document everything that's known from the first great Martian war.' She laid it out on the table and the three senior servicemen gathered round, fumbling in pockets for reading glasses. Once these had been located, they looked on with interest at Ellen turned the pages. 'Here you all are,' she announced as they reached the pages set on the Moon, and as Mrs Tickle, sans space suit, jumped up to join them at the table, she added, 'and your lovely cats of course.' The men, and cat, purred with recognition. Feeling some memories of that distant time being nurtured in their brain. 'And here is the page where the Martians appear to be defeated, there's these gas canisters that, supposedly, send the foe to sleep, but what's actually in them, I have no idea.' Trout leaned forward to look and one of the other cats, as yet introduced, pawed keenly at his arm.

'What's that Marvin? Ah yes, well I'll certainly tell her,' he responded to the cat's insistent signal.

'Tell her what?' enquired Cleanta also leaning in curiously.

'Well we've got loads of those canisters in our storage, we wondered what they might be for.'

'Oh my goodness, really?' exclaimed Ellen.

'Yes, odd thing really, any time we sent anyone to look into what they might be the chap wouldn't be seen for days. When we finally found them, they'd have no memory of even going to look at them. Most peculiar.' Ellen jumped up from the table at this revelation and snapped her fingers.

'By Jove I think that's it! We've nothing to lose, let's get a few canisters and try it on our Martian chums. Only let's make sure we have our spacesuits on when we do it.' There were no dissenting voices.

Despite their age, the venerable soldiers of the Albion Expeditionary Force (Extra-terrestrial) knew how to organise a military operation. Taking extra precautions to make sure no humans, or cats, came in direct contact with the sickly brown gas, the canisters were retrieved from dusty storage and released wherever the Martians could be found in enclosed spaces. The results were satisfying and exhilarating in equal measures as the three-eyed foes were found to be induced into a deep comatose state by the emanation, from which they showed no signs of recovery.

Emboldened by this discovery, under cover of the Lunar night, a small group of commandos, led by Cleanta and Trout, with Ellen in close attendance sneaked their way into the first of the Martian's three colossal interplanetary rockets and released two full canisters.

Heartened by the sleeping aliens, but always nagged by the anxious thought that no one else had yet followed them up via the EAR-MOO, Ellen and Cleanta vowed to continue to the other rockets without rest and finish the main mission, before finding some way to return to Earth and explain the, newly realised, solution to their fellow Albioners. Things went well on the second rocket, but by the third the Martians had become aware of their presence and a fierce firefight broke out. The Space Commandos fought valiantly, given their age, and the final canisters were released without any human casualties. However, as she observed the final Martians fall into a deep slumber, Ellen watched in horror, through the thick brown gas, as Cleanta took a wild shot to her arm and fell clutching a rent in her spacesuit. Without really thinking of her own safety, she rushed to her side, absentmindedly taking off her helmet as she did so.

'Cleanta, are you okay?' she enquired urgently putting pressure on her arm although she was relieved to see that no blood was leaking into the heavy cotton and leather sleeve.

'I'm okay, just a nick. Gosh, I am so very tired,' responded Cleanta seemingly a little disorientated. 'Help me take this helmet off.' Ellen moved to obey her as the gas continued to clear. 'Where are we?'

'I'm not really sure,' stated Ellen, looking around blankly at the corridor which seemed empty of any other souls.

'In the pirate base I guess,' muttered Cleanta, who seemed to be drifting off to sleep. 'I'm just so exhausted.'

'I know what you mean,' agreed Ellen, feeling the exertions of the last few days suddenly catching up with her. 'I guess they won't mind if we take a nap, I'm sure they'll come and get us if they get the EAR-MOO working.'

'What's an EAR-MOO?' mumbled Cleanta before her eyes drifted shut and she fell asleep. All around them there was a dull rumble, which seemed oddly comforting.

'Oh, I'll tell you later,' soothed Ellen, settling herself down. 'I certainly know what you mean about being tired. Let's grab forty winks and then we can catch up properly. It's just so good to see you again, and...'

She never completed her sentence as with that they both drifted into an uneasy, but long overdue sleep.

Little were they to know that, as he succumbed to the brown gas and drifted into a coma, a junior Martian pilot had fallen onto the emergency recall button. This was a failsafe mechanism designed to launch the rocket back into the void and return the incumbents to whence they had come, in case of dire emergency. It probably should have had its cover closed, but you know how pilots get when they have little to do. And so, blissfully unaware of anything that had happened in the last day, Ellen and Cleanta fell asleep in each other's arms, on an alien rocket leaving the relative confines of the Moon and taking them, and their sleeping Martian companions, to the distant red planet known to all in New Albion as Mars.

The End?

After The Words, Some More Words

I have literally just finished the first draft of the story above (XX) and I thought that after making your way through two volumes of my ramblings, that you might be interested to know something of why these stories exist, and why they are the way they are.

Firstly though (excuse my manners) thank you. Thank you for buying this tome and, presumably, the previous tome also. There is little point in my having spent the last umpteen years of my life tormenting myself over these stories if no one actually reads them. So, from the bottom of my heart, thank you. I probably don't need to tell you, as I expect it's all too obvious, but this is not a steampunk novel. Or indeed a Novella due to its length. No indeed, it's very much a collection of short stories, that may, or may not be connected. Some background might be useful here.

For many years I laboured under the misapprehension that I could write a novel. Everyone thinks they have one in them, and I was convinced I had several. Much starting, with not a lot of finishing, later I gave up on the whole idea and went off to become either a rock musician, a t-shirt salesman or an IT consultant, depending on whom you ask. Nevertheless, I did dabble with the occasional piece of writing, and certainly my imagination did not let up as it continued to supply me with a non-stop stream of crazy ideas. Indeed, one morning I awoke from sleep with what seemed to be an entire story in my head. The genre of said tale seemed to fall into the category of "Steampunk" something I was vaguely aware of, but had never come across in the flesh, as it were. Thinking that I should do something more than just park it under "what could have been" I mentioned it to a certain Ben Henderson, whom I understood knew more about these steamy-punky things than I did. He was very encouraging and convinced me to write the story down with the aim, no less, of reading it at one of his Steampunk gatherings, or Convivials as he called them. So, with no little trepidation, this is what I did. That story turned out to be (after a couple of name changes – Futureshock, for example, being already in use by 2000AD) *Timeshock* which forms the very first story of this saga. All the characters in that story were literally made up off the top of my head, and inserted into this - dreamt up - story as they occurred to me. I had no thought of doing any more, but a seed, it seemed, had been sown. Ben asked me back to do another reading, so another story was necessary. I rummaged around in my brain looking for something interesting to add to this Victorian(ish) world I had created, but no obvious contenders could be found. I had in the back of my mind the idea to use a story I had first written age 12 about a desperate man who keeps seeing people who seem to mysteriously vanish. The story had held my Prestwood Middle School class so entranced that I realised that it was worth hanging on to. I'd then rewritten it for a Puffin Book Club competition as a Sci-Fi story and received a Highly Commended award. This seemed like a good banker story if nothing else came to me, and could easily be adapted into the Steampunk world, so I wrote a third version of it. That story is *Tobias Fitch*. In order to write this story, I found it necessary to get out of the house and the distractions of the internet, so ended up writing at our local café – The Coffee Station, near Portslade Railway Station. This building is an odd affair with a coffee shop on one corner and doorways and extensions on the other side. It planted the germ of another idea. What if a café had been built into a cliff and then other restaurants built all around it, with all the ancillary services, until the original establishment had been subsumed by them all and lost to memory? This train of thought gave rise to *The High Cliffs Tea Room* and, coincidentally gave me an opportunity to give a backstory to Ellen Hall.

And so, it went on. Each story was created in order to be read at a Surrey Steampunk Convivial and was created in a mad panic during the weeks leading up to the events. Somehow an idea always came to me, and the story would be written. New characters and places would emerge, and some familiar ones would return. As each was finished though, I had not the faintest idea of where the story might go next, I was simply relieved to have something worth sharing with other folk. The formats also shifted a little as I got more experienced. For a start I made them shorter. It was fine to stick six or seven thousand words down on paper, but reading that out in one sitting was a tall order. Trust me, even a sympathetic audience is not used, these days, to sitting still for the best part of an hour listening to a story. Nevertheless, a few people did listen, and the stories kept coming, albeit latterly at about three to four thousand words, which is much more manageable and takes about half an hour to read. It's also why these stories tend to come across as radio monologues rather than the usual short stories you might expect in an anthology.

So, my process became this: think desperately of a story and try and form it in my mind with three acts: beginning, middle and end. Then, with deadline looming, get out of the house and write. Usually this was to The Coffee Station (over two Americanos) or latterly to The Garden Bar in Hove (over three medium glasses of Sauvignon Blanc) where the first draft would be completed as best I could. Finally, I would read it aloud to make sure it was ready for a performance. This process of thought, typing and reading seems to tick all the boxes for me and combining this with short stories of five thousand words or less meant that I suddenly found I was six or seven stories into a collection. Along the way I finally relaxed enough to play around with the format a little. A request for a Christmas performance needed a Christmas story, and since I'd always loved A Christmas Carol, it was natural that I might try my hand a Steampunk version. That Scrooge should turn out to be the one who loved Christmas all along, and then changed his mind, seemed like the only viable road to take.

Although I said that I never knew what was coming next when I wrote each story, this is not strictly true of the end of volume one. I realised at some point that ten stories seemed a good round number to put together in a book and with three left to go, I decided there should be some attempt to round off the first volume in a less random way than had occurred up until then. So, I conceived the idea of three chapters that told the same story from different viewpoints, and that the order should be wrong. So that is why 2 and 3 come before 1. Despite the numbering I wrote them in the order they appear in the book (as with every single story to date, they are presented in the order written). Writing the last few lines of *In The Shadow Of The Moon* reduced me to tears, and that's true pretty much every time I attempt to read them. But hey, the book was done. With artwork by the supremely talented Frog Morris to adorn it, I delved into the murky world of Amazon publishing and pressed all the right buttons to unleash *Tales of New Albion* on an unsuspecting world in 2017. I was glad I did, otherwise I might have procrastinated forever. Turns out though the book was riddled with literary garbage and so, a much revised, and quite frankly all-round better product, was uploaded in 2018 which is the version you can purchase now. If you have one of the 1st Editions I strongly recommend you burn it.

You'd think that might be quite enough of that, but the world of New Albion seems reluctant to let me go. At some point it occurred to me, or someone suggested it, I forget which, that I might make a good radio show... so the Tales of New Albion podcast was born. For this I needed original music, so my lovely (and also far more talented) wife – Charlie – came up with an amazing ten tune soundtrack album which we mastered at Hafod Mastering in Wales. The stories continued to come, and for fun, I set myself different challenges. That is why, in this very book, you will have come across a one man play with eighteen characters and a couple of chapters that are, supposedly, extracts from autobiographical works. I really do hope it all makes some sort of sense. I think it vaguely does. Anyway, but now you'll know the fate of Ellen (who has become a bit of a favourite character, don't tell the others, I really do love them all to bits) and her, erm, "friend" Cleanta, but whether I ever write another story in this universe is uncertain. In a way it's really up to you. Do you want to hear more? Do you want to know what happens next? Well then, let me know via letters@talesofnewalbion.com. I'm sure there are a thousand more stories to be told (well another ten at least), perhaps you might even have some ideas? Until that time though, thank you, once again, for reading right to the end. Now you're finished, why not pass it on to a friend, write me a review, or just pour another cup of tea/something stronger and start reading again right from the start. You might be able to tell me what I got wrong. I'm sure there is loads. Anyway, did I say thank you?

From the top, bottom, middle and sides of my heart, I thank you.

Daren Callow, *a medium-sized cannon shot from the English Channel.*

Also by this Author

Tales of New Albion – Volume 1

Tales of New Albion podcast

Plus, short stories in:

Elements of Horror, Book One: Earth
Elements of Horror, Book Two: Air
Elements of Horror, Book Three: Fire
Elements of Horror, Book Four: Water

Printed in Poland
by Amazon Fulfillment
Poland Sp. z o.o., Wrocław